CARSON KETTLE U. S. MARSHAL BOOK 4

WYATT COCHRANE

Copyright © 2021 by Wyatt Cochrane

All rights reserved.

No part of this book may be reproduced in any form or by any electronic or mechanical means, including information storage and retrieval systems, without written permission from the author, except for the use of brief quotations in a book review.

To the courageous women and men of law enforcement I had the privilege of working with over the years.

1

Carson stirred. A dull ache radiated from his shoulder, up his neck, and down his arm. His first cloudy thought was to open his eyes, but the lids hung reluctant and heavy. Somewhere, not too close by, a woman hummed, and there was a scratching sound. He fought through the thick brain fog. What was the sound and where was he? A metal pen nib on paper. He was sure of it. But where and why? He closed his dry mouth and scraped his tongue over the parched roof, tasting something, rank, something akin to decaying flesh. He worked enough slick moisture from beneath his tongue to swallow down some of the bitterness. A sweet, tarry, medicinal smell filled his nose.

As his thoughts inched into clearer focus, the desire, to see where he was, filled him. He raised his eyelids, but something held them closed. He reached up with his right hand to wipe them clean. The dull pain in his shoulder turned to fire.

He remembered.

Patricia Grimwald had shot him.

He sucked in a breath and eased his left hand to his eyes

and scraped away the crust gumming his lashes together. After blinking several times, a whitewashed ceiling came into focus. He'd been here before. But when?

Moving only his eyes, he glanced around the room. It all came flooding back. His bullets hitting Patricia and her father. Their house in flames... and Bella!

He threw off the light sheet, twisted on the cot, and dropped his feet to the floor. Pain shot through him, and the room swirled. He bit back a groan. Holding his right arm tight against his ribs, he leaned forward and stood, his entire body trembled, and his weak legs threatened to buckle.

The humming stopped, and the door burst open. "You're awake," Nancy, Mr. Cadwallader's assistant, said. She covered her mouth and backed out the door and slammed it shut. "Cover yourself."

Carson glanced down and indeed, his pale, thin body was naked. He looked around and found his clothes, washed, mended, and folded on the seat of one of the two straight-backed wooden chairs in the room. He staggered over and picked up his red union suit with his left hand. As he tried to raise a leg and step into the underwear, his head spun, and he tumbled onto the hard, polished-plank floor.

Mr. Cadwallader, the Quaker Indian agent, burst through the door. "What art thou doing?" He turned and looked over his shoulder. "Nancy. Go fetch the doctor.... And the major." Shaking his head, he turned back to Carson. "Let's get thee back into bed."

Carson fought through the pain shooting from his right shoulder. "Where's Bella?"

The red-faced cavalry doctor rushed into the room. "What happened?"

Mr. Cadwallader grabbed Carson by the left bicep and began to lift. "He fell."

Carson jerked his arm free. "I can get up myself." He rolled onto his knees and pressed his hand against the seat of the chair holding his clothes.

The doctor stepped behind him and grabbed him under the arms. "Let me help you."

Carson twisted. "I can do it."

"You tear open that wound, and you'll wish you took some help," the young doctor said. "Now let us help you!"

Carson stopped struggling.

Major Kinsey threw open the door. He smiled. "Glad to see you're still with us, Deputy. I didn't know how I was going to explain my getting you killed out here to Marshal Greer. How's he look, Doc?"

The doctor unrolled the last of the bandage, eased the pad away from the front of Carson's shoulder, and held it to his nose. He thrust it up toward the major.

The major jerked back his head and grinned. "Just tell me."

"Infection's gone," the doctor said. He laid his palm on Carson's forehead. "And the fever's broken." He smiled at Carson. "Looks like you're going to live."

Carson glanced around the room. "What day is it?"

"It's the Sabbath," Mr. Cadwallader said.

Sunday? He'd ridden back to the fort from the Grimwald's ranch on Tuesday. And Bella's wagon was already gone then. At least five days.

The major nodded. "Phillip sent word. She's taking the girls to him."

Carson's sluggish mind churned. Phillip had run off and left Bella and his daughters. How would Bella find him? And why would she...? "You let her go alone, with the girls?"

"Of course not," the major said. "I sent Gate and a couple of troopers to escort her back to the California Road."

Carson started to rise, but the doctor held him down. "Why would you let her go?" Carson said. "Phillip's gone. He didn't send for her."

The major straightened his back. "I assure you he did. She showed me the letter and the gold eagles he sent her."

Deputy Marty Dunnegan burst into the room, a huge grin splitting his freckled face. "You're awake! We can finally head home. ...What's wrong?"

"Bella's run off. I have to go after her."

Marty glanced from Carson to the major and back. "What do you mean go after her. Gate hooked her up with that wagon train. Her and old Phillip's likely married and halfway to El Paso by now."

Carson leaned over and pulled on the red union suit, still hanging from one of his ankles. He looked up at Marty. "Bring me my trousers."

The doctor placed a firm hand on Carson's shoulder. "It's too soon for you to go anywhere. You need at least another week."

Carson thrust the doctor's hand aside. "She's not thinking clearly. If I ride straight south, I can cut her off at Fort Belknap."

An hour later, Carson pulled with his left arm and struggled into his saddle. He turned the sorrel toward Marty. "Tell the Marshal, I'll be back as soon as I can."

Marty scowled. "I don't understand why you're doing this."

"There's things I know that you don't. Things I can't share. Just tell the Marshal."

"You're in no shape to ride alone. Let me get saddled."

Carson reined the sorrel south. "This is mine to do. You head back to Fort Smith. Tell the marshal what happened out here. I'll head back there as soon as I find Bella and the girls"

Marty nodded. "Alright."

Gate rode a big bay horse around the corner of the stable. "Deputies."

"Gate," Carson said, as he started the sorrel south.

Gate trotted up beside him.

After a hundred yards without a word, Carson said, "Don't try to stop me. This is something I have to do."

Gate raised the corners of his mouth. "I'm not trying to stop you. I'm coming with you."

Carson pulled the sorrel to a stop. "Coming with me? Why? Just go back. I don't need a nursemaid."

Gate raised one eyebrow. "That so?"

"That's so," Carson said.

"I had a bad feeling about sending Bella and the children off with that wagon train, but I know the wagon master, and he gave me his word, he'll look after them. "

"So why are you coming?"

"Besides the fact the major told me to, I guess I want to make sure she's alright. I don't cotton to that Phillip."

Carson didn't have the strength to argue, so he just started the sorrel toward the Red River.

Before they'd covered a mile, Sergeant Alf Buckley galloped over a hill and caught them. He still wore his turned-up cavalry hat, but instead of his uniform, he wore canvas trousers and a faded yellow shirt.

"I already told Gate, I'm not turning back," Carson said, as Alf rode alongside.

"That's why I'm coming with you," Alf said with a grin. "You don't think I'd let you boyos have all the fun, do you? Now that we stopped the war., the others can find those stolen horses. Besides, things are about to get all spit and polish at the fort, and that's a good time to be out riding."

IT WAS all Carson could do to stay in the saddle by the time they topped the rise overlooking the Grimwald's ranch. He stopped his sorrel.

A couple of ranch hands loafed around the yard, but the big old ranch house was gone, burned completely to the ground.

"My oh my," Alf said. "I always liked that house." He smiled. "You don't suppose the boys got the whiskey out of the cellar before everything crashed in?"

Carson was too tired to reply and Gate too serious.

Alf eased his horse ahead. "Let's find out."

Carson reined his horse west. "I won't be welcome there. Not after Patricia and Mr. Grimwald and Britt and …."

Gate followed him.

"All right then," Alf said. "I suppose you're right. They probably didn't save the whiskey anyway."

Carson led them to the spring where he had a week earlier, fought and killed Britt Viola. There was fresh water and wood there.

At the spring, Carson more fell, than climbed off his horse. Using his left hand, he loosened the cinch.

Alf stepped in behind him. "Let me do that."

"I'm fine. I'll take care of it."

"You're not fine. Go sit down before you fall down."

Carson started to argue, but his aching shoulder and the trembling in his legs convinced him Alf was right. He bowed his head. "Thank you. I appreciate it."

Leaned against a big cottonwood, he watched Alf and

Gate tend to the horses. He glanced at the spot where Britt Viola had gasped his last breaths. What made men so different? Why did men like Britt believe that they could take whatever they wanted, and usually did, while others like Mr. Cadwallader lived on almost nothing and spent their time helping others?

Alf lit a fire and pulled bacon and beans from his saddlebags. Before long, the smell of the bacon frying, beans bubbling, and coffee boiling filled the air. Carson's mouth watered. He pushed himself to his feet. "Let me tend that. It's the least I can do."

Alf smiled and handed Carson his fork. Moments later he returned with plates and cups.

Once the food was ready, Carson took his plate full and leaned back against the tree. He had picked at his breakfast at the fort, and nibbled on a little jerky at midday, but this evening his appetite had come roaring back. He sopped up every drop of sweet bean juice from his plate, then took another biscuit and wiped it around the unwashed pot.

Alf turned to Gate. "Looks like our deputy's got his appetite back."

Gate nodded without smiling. "Guess we'll have to stop at Eagle Flat and every other post along the way, if that keeps up."

Alf grinned and winked at Carson. He stood and walked to his saddlebags. "I don't mind stopping. I get tired of eating jackrabbits on the trail." He glanced over his shoulder. "Look here. I even brought us some dessert."

Carson hoped Alf had brought cake or pie from the dining hall, but instead, he stood up with a bottle of Irish whiskey. He pulled the cork with his teeth and took a long pull straight from the bottle, before handing it to Gate. He stood waiting, while Gate drank, then took the bottle and handed it to Carson.

Carson took a sip. Though almost as smooth flavored as Mr. Grimwald's bourbon, the whiskey burned its way down Carson's abused throat and sat smoldering in his belly.

Alf refused the bottle when Carson handed it back. "Drink like a man," he said.

Carson really didn't feel like more whiskey, but it seemed easier to drink than to argue, so he took a healthy swallow. By the time he handed the bottle back, his head had already begun to swim, and his stomach churned.

When Alf came back around with the bottle, Carson held out his palm. "Tastes good, but no more for me."

Alf stood holding the bottle toward Carson, then chuckled and said, "Leaves more for me and Old Gate." He shrugged, tipped the bottle back, and took two big swallows.

The horses raised their heads. Gate picked up his rifle.

"What is it?" Carson asked.

Gate rolled over onto his knees and peeked around the tree he sat against.

"Carson Kettle," a man called from the darkness.

Carson peered out and tried to see who it was, but he had been staring into the fire and was night blind.

"Is that you, Horace?" Gate asked.

"This is between me and the deputy," Horace said. "I've got no grievance with either of the other of you two."

"What do you want?" Carson asked.

"I could have bushwhacked you all. I saw you looking down at the ranch," Horace said. "We followed you out here."

"Why?" Carson asked.

"For Miss Patricia," Horace replied. He stepped into the flickering firelight, a cocked pistol in his hand, and his red-rimmed eyes burning with rage. He glanced over his shoulder. "You boys shoot 'em if any of them move and I don't tell 'em to."

"I didn't want to kill her," Carson said. "I wanted to take her in, and let the judge decide. She left me no choice."

Horace motioned with his cocked Colt. "Get up."

"Don't do this, Horace," Alf said. "You won't walk away from here, you pull that trigger."

"You let Horace have the deputy and we won't shoot you, soldier boy, or you, Gate Rudd," a voice called from the darkness.

Carson pushed to his feet. He nodded toward his gun belt hanging from the stump of a broken branch near where Horace stood. "I'm unarmed. This will be cold-blooded murder."

Horace swiped at the corner of his eye with his left hand. "That's what you deserve, but I'll let you strap on your gun, then I'll holster mine. We'll let God sort it out."

"He's shot," Alf said. "He can hardly use his right arm. Look at him, man."

Horace smiled and motioned with his pistol. "Git to it. Strap it on."

Carson's heart pounded against his breastbone as he stepped toward his own pistol. He rolled his right shoulder and flexed his fingers. Could he even draw, let alone aim and shoot? He glanced away from Horace and met Gate's eyes, then he glanced at Alf. Both men looked tight as coiled spring and ready for action.

Horace moved in behind as Carson stepped close to the tree and reached for his gun belt. There was no way he could draw with his right hand, and even if he buckled his belt on with the pistol on the left, it would be butt-first and there would be zero chance of beating Horace to the draw.

"You going to let me buckle it on first?" Carson said, as he lifted the gun belt from the branch.

As Horace began to speak, Carson spun on one foot and swung his heavy Colt into Horace's jaw.

Horace's pistol fired at the same time his eyes rolled back into his head, and Carson dropped to his belly and rolled in behind the tree.

Rifle fire and streaks of flame filled the night air. Carson cocked his Colt with his left thumb, and when the rifle fire stopped, rolled on his belly until he could see past the tree.

Gate and Alf had disappeared.

Horace stirred then looked around with wild eyes.

"Don't you move," Carson said.

Horace's eyes found his own pistol, inches from his outstretched hand. He roared and grabbed for the Colt. As his fingers closed around the butt, Carson shouted. "I said don't move."

Horace ignored him and raised and cocked the weapon.

Carson's bullet tore through Horace's neck and burst out in a spray of blood and bone.

The Colt fell to the ground, and Horace dropped, face-first, onto the grass.

Thundering hooves marked horses galloping off into the night.

"Want me to go after him?" Gate shouted, from where he was hidden in the underbrush.

"They all gone?" Carson asked.

"One dead, one gone," Gate replied. "Sounds like he took all the horses with him."

"Let him go," Carson said.

2

A cold wind tugged at Carson's blankets. Above, dark clouds boiled from east to west. He closed his eyes, pulled the wool blanket up over his chin, and ignored the scratch of the rough fibers. Normally a little wind like this wouldn't chill him to the bone this way. He needed to regain his strength.

Across the clearing and the fire pit, the horses stood, tails to the wind, nibbling at the grass. Beyond the horses, the bodies of Horace and a young ranch hand, Carson had seen but never spoken to lay side by side.

Beside him, Alf snored, his head hanging straight back over his saddle.

He glanced at the big sergeant, then struggled out of his blanket and tarp and pushed himself to his feet using his left hand.

He unknotted his bandana, used it to pick up the pot sitting on a bed of glowing coals, and poured thick, burnt-smelling coffee into two of the three cups sitting next to the fire ring.

"Gate?" he said, just above a whisper.

Gate cleared his throat from a spot to Carson's left.

"Brought you some coffee."

"Over here," Gate said.

"Anybody about?"

"Nope."

Gate blew across the mug then sipped the hot brew. "It ain't time to spell me, and besides, I told you we'd watch. You need some rest."

"Can't sleep."

Gate nodded as if he understood.

They sat sipping coffee and listening to the insects buzzing and the faint cries of two distant mockingbirds.

Carson wrapped his hands around the cup and warmed them. "Did she say anything?"

Gate took a deep breath. "Bella? Not really, but you know I'm not much for conversation."

"Why would she go? I asked her to wait until I came back."

"She said that lazy Phillip sent her a letter and some money and asked her to bring his girls."

"Do you believe that?"

"Seemed unlikely, since the old boy they sent to fort for a few supplies didn't tell anyone but her. But I'd never call that girl a liar. Not after watching her with those girls and never after what she's been through. She had gold coins to pay her way."

Carson cleared his throat. "That's not what I meant... I mean.... Well, what I think is she's running away, and taking those girls before Cadwallader and the major decided to send them to an orphanage."

The full moon broke through an opening in the dark clouds, casting pale light over them. "She do love those girls," Gate said, "And they love her." He narrowed his eyebrows and his lips almost disappeared. "I'm afraid I might do that Phillip harm if'n I see him again."

Carson took one last sip and tossed the rest of his coffee onto the ground. "You and me both. You sure she didn't say anything about where she was going?"

"Not to me, but I overheard when she told Clifford she was going to California to teach school, just like her daddy and her dead husband had planned."

"Dead husband?"

Gate shook his head. "Don't ask me. Not my place to question her or to set her story straight, but I noticed she were wearing a wedding band."

Carson scratched his chin. "Who's Clifford?"

"Clifford Van Zant. He's the wagon boss. Cliff's a little rough around the edges, but there's none better on the trail. Known him for years. Them girls is in good hands. They're taking the southern route and there's no one better than Clifford to take them. Far as I can see, that Phillip leaving was the best thing coulda happened to them."

Carson waited for Gate to continue, but the scout had said more than he intended, and he looked away and out into the darkness.

Carson sighed and did the same. What was he doing? She left even though he'd asked her to wait. It seemed obvious that she wanted nothing more to do with him, but maybe there was more to her story, and how could he possibly figure out her reasons, when he didn't even know what he wanted of her or of himself?

∽

SUNLIGHT TICKLED the treetops and found Carson staring up at the fluttering leaves. He glanced at Gate sleeping nearby, then eased out of his bedroll. He added a handful of tinder to the fire and was about to blow the fire to life, when someone cocked a pistol. He dropped to his bottom and pushed back with his legs toward his own Colt, hanging near his bedroll.

"Oh," Gate said, uncocking his weapon. "It's you." He glanced at the sky, dropped back against his blanket, tucked his pistol in along his leg, and closed his eyes. Within seconds, his breath returned to its long, slow rhythm.

Once the sun had crested the trees around the spring, Alf came in from his guard post. "Bacon smells good. Did you make a fresh pot?"

Carson nodded and poured a cup of steaming black brew and held it toward Alf.

Gate rolled up his bedroll and pulled on his boots.

Carson yawned as he lifted the skillet from the fire and set it on a flat rock. He poured two more cups of coffee. "Once we eat, I guess we'll bury those two and get moving.

Alf laughed. "And by we, you mean Gate and I."

"I'll help," Carson said.

"Not with that broken wing of yours."

"Leave them," Gate said. "That cowboy that run off last night can come back and tend to 'em."

Carson looked to Alf for support, then he glanced at the sky. Three wide-winged buzzards circled. "Let's at least cover them with branches or something."

Gate pressed his lips together but held his tongue.

Alf said, "Let's eat first."

Once they'd eaten and covered the bodies with branches, Gate climbed onto his horse. "We'd best ride if'n we want to get to the falls before that wagon train. They've a good head start.

BELLA ROCKED with the sway of the wagon. Already tired of sitting day in and day out on the hard wooden wagon seat, she longed for the days when her dear father had done most of the driving and she'd been free to run and play with Phillip's girls. She brought her hands holding the thick, oiled leather lines, together and touch the thin gold band on her left ring finger with the pinky of her right hand. What was she doing? Her mother, if she were looking down, would be ashamed of all the lying. Or would she?

She remembered the day young Garrett Kris had stolen an apple from the basket at the front of Burger's store. Old Mr. Burger shouted, "Stop! Thief!"

Garret darted across the street and glanced up at Bella with a cheeky, apple-filled grin on his face, at least until he ran into the arms of Mr. David Tucker. Mr. Burger leaned into his store and came out with a harness strap. He waddled across the street, the brass buckle hanging, its prong clinking with every stride.

Garrett's grin fled and he jerked and struggled and twisted, but Mr. Tucker held tight.

The first swing of the belt struck Garrett's shoulder.

Bella wanted to do something, beg Mr. Burger to stop, but her feet seemed frozen to the boardwalk and her tongue to the roof of her mouth.

At the next swing, Garret twisted and tried to duck away.

The heavy buckle slammed across the boy's cheek, its rough corner scraping the skin. Bright blood appeared where a moment before there was only dirty, sun-browned skin.

Again, Mr. Burger cocked back his arm, but before he could swing, Bella's mother leaped off the boardwalk, grabbed the buckle, and shouted, "Stop! It was only an apple."

Mr. Burger's already red face, turned purple, and he turned as if he were about to strike Bella's mother.

"Burger," Mr. Tucker shouted. "She's right. It was only an apple."

Burger lowered the strap, locked eyes with Bella's mother, and snorted. "It weren't the first one he's took."

Bella's mother held the angry man's gaze while she fumbled in her reticule for a coin. "His father's sick. You know that. How much for the apple?"

"Two for a nickel," Burger said. "But that ain't the point."

She held out a quarter. "How many will that buy"

Mr. Burger hesitated.

"Ten," Bella's mother said. "And here's another. That makes twenty. When that runs out, you let me know." She turned to Garrett. "You, young man, need to get to school, but you come and see me at the house as soon as it lets out."

Garrett, one hand on his bloody cheek, the other clutching the bitten apple, kicked the ground and said, "Yes, ma'am."

Mr. Tucker let go of the boy's collar, and he scampered off toward the schoolhouse.

The right front wheel of the wagon ran over a big rock and jerked Bella back to the present.

Gemma trotted over and bounded up onto the seat beside Bella. "What's wrong?"

Bella took the lines in one hand and wrapped her other

arm around the pretty, dark-eyed, tall girl. "I'm alright. I was just remembering my sweet momma."

Gemma's smile faded. She wrapped both arms around Bella's waist. "I love you."

Bella pulled her even closer. "I love you too."

A tall man, wearing a black and white skunk fur cap, rode past the wagon. He pulled his hand from the hide of the gutted whitetail doe hanging over the front of his saddle, touched the side of the hat and nodded. "How are you ladies making out?"

Bella looked up and smiled. "We're doing just fine, Mr. Van Zant. Thank you again for letting us join you."

He ran a hand down his red and mostly gray beard, showing his blood and dirt caked fingernails. "Good to hear. You have any trouble you get word to me."

Bella nodded, grateful that Mr. Gate Rudd, one of her saviors, had spoken up for her and vouched for this rough spoken man.

"We'll stop in about an hour. I'll send that Harker boy to help you."

"That won't be necessary," Bella said, but Mr. Van Zant had already ridden away.

An hour later, when Mr. Van Zant called it a day, Bella followed the wagon ahead of her into the large circle the thirty wagons of the train formed. When the wagon ahead of her stopped, she reined her team to the outside of the circle and set the brake.

With Gemma's help, she managed to unhitch the team and drive them clear of the wagon tongue. As she struggled to roll the heavy leather work harness from the near horse, a hearty voice called out. "Let me do that, Mrs. Foresti."

Bella glanced at the blonde-haired, gangly young man striding toward her. "No need Vern. We can handle it."

He lowered his eyes and his cheeks reddened. "It's really no problem. In fact, you'd be doing a favor it you'd let me help. I wouldn't dare tell Mr. Van Zant I let you ladies do it yourself."

"That's right," Van Zant said with a chuckle in his voice.

"Sorry Mr. Van Zant," Vern said. "I didn't hear you, coming."

"You'd best learn to listen before we get to that Colorado River country or a renegade Comache'll have that pretty yellow hair." He turned and winked at Gemma. "Miss Gemma. I want you and your sisters to sneak up on this boy every chance you get."

Gemma's neck and cheeks flushed bright red. She lowered her head hiding her eyes behind the brim of her bonnet. "Yes, sir. We will."

Mr. Van Zant dropped one of the haunches of the doe he'd shot on the seat of Bella's wagon. "Might want to salt and cook most of this, so it don't spoil. You got a big pot?"

Bella nodded. "I do, and thank you Mr. Van Zant. Would you join us for supper?"

Van Zant looked at Vern. "Usually eat with the Harkers, and that bunch, but I suppose I might like a change, or they might. Right Vern?"

Vern and Gemma stood close to one another, shyly glancing back and forth and smiling.

"I said, right Vern Harker."

Vern jerked his eyes from Gemma. "Yes, sir. That's right."

"Would you like to join us too, Vern?" Bella asked.

Vern beamed. "Oh, yes ma'am. Yes, I would. I'd best get these horses tended to, then I'll go and tell my folks. Or maybe I'll see if my ma wants y'all to come eat with us."

Mr. Van Zant's smile fled. "Let's eat over here, just for now, Vern."

"Yes, sir," Vern said, as he trotted away.

A tall, thin man, with deep-set, dark eyes and dark hair brushing his shoulders, rode past. The long, red-brown hair above the horse's hooves bounced as the big feet thudded against the ground, kicking up puffs of dirt.

The man tucked the long-barreled shotgun, he carried, under his arm and tipped his hat. He smiled, but there was no warmth in it, and Bella fought the urge to turn away.

3
___

The smell of onions and rich venison mixed with the wood smoke of the fire, filled the air. Bella took a flour sack towel and lifted the heavy pot from the hook hanging by a chain from the center of the iron tripod she had placed over the fire. She set the pot on the tailgate of the wagon, lifted the lid, and tasted the bubbling venison stew. A little bland, she sprinkled in two healthy pinches of salt.

She glanced at the Dutch oven nestled in a bed of coals at the edge of the fire, and was about to pull it off, when Gemma trotted up. "Are the biscuits ready? I'll get them."

Bella winked and smiled. "What's got into you today?"

Gemma blushed. "Nothing. I just want to help you."

Bella handed her the towel. "I'm sure they're ready. Careful you don't burn yourself."

Gemma looked up from the heavy pot she carried, as Mr. Van Zant marched past the front of the wagon, a tin plate, coffee cup and spoon in hand. He touched his skunk-fur hat and grinned. "Smells just fine, Mrs. Foresti."

"Everything's ready. Should we wait for Vern?"

Mr. Van Zant looked back. "He won't be joining us. His ma had something for him to do."

Gemma's smile fled.

Bella saw the disappointment in the girl's eyes and her heart hurt. This had nothing to do with the young people. She'd felt the disapproval from the other women of the wagon train from the first day, they had joined. Though no one had said anything, Bella saw how the other women looked away when she passed by. She didn't care a whit what they thought of her, but it hurt when they whisked their children away whenever her girls, yes, now they were hers, tried to make conversation or join in the evening play.

She snapped her head toward Mr. Van Zant. "I'm sorry. I didn't hear what you said."

He leaned in close and spoke softly. "Don't mind those old biddies. They's just afraid one of their men'll take a shine to you and toss them aside." He grinned. "Truth be told, I wouldn't blame them if they did, but there ain't a one of them old boys you'd want. Don't worry, they'll come around 'fore we get to Californy. And if they don't, the better for you."

Bella forced a smile. "Gemma, call your sisters. It's time to eat."

Mr. Van Zant had a second and a third helping of the stew. He finally sat back and said, "That was mighty fine."

Bella smiled. "That fresh venison made all the difference." She turned to the girls. "Liliana. Please bring the cobbler. Gemma, dear, bring the sugar."

Bella and girls finished their cobbler and watched while Mr. Van Zant sprinkled two heaping teaspoons of sugar over the remaining peaches and biscuit dough and polished it off. He sat back and smiled. "That was fine, Mrs. Foresti." He pushed his palms against his knees and stood up from the stump he sat on. "A word, ma'am."

Bella turned to the girls. "You ladies clean up tonight."

The four girls moaned in unison, but Bella gave them her sternest look, and Gemma took charge.

At the edge of the lantern light, Mr. Van Zant pulled off his hat and wrung it in his hands. His pale bald pate shone in the lantern light.

Bella's chest tightened and she said a silent prayer. "Please don't let this be what I think it is."

Mr. Van Zant cleared his throat. "Well. It's just that." He looked over her shoulder toward the girls. "Well, you see, I was hoping I could join you and the girls for all my meals."

Bella's shoulders fell, and the air she'd been holding escaped.

"I'd keep you in meat and buy my share of staples, of course. It's well..., that was a fine meal and I enjoy the girls and well, you're mighty pleasant to be around. Fact is..."

Bella's breathing stopped again. She was just about to lie again and tell him she still grieved for her dear departed husband, when he said, "I lost my wife and daughter. Seems like a lifetime ago. Fact is, my girl would be around your age now, if the fever hadn't took 'em, and I'd like to think she'd be as fine as you."

Bella touched his arm. "We'd love to have you eat with us."

THE HITCHING RAIL in front of the trading post narrowed and widened as if beavers had been at it. Carson doubted it would hold a determined pony if something spooked it, let alone the half-dozen cavalry mounts already tied there, and their three horses. The sorrel had never pulled back, so he wrapped his reins around a spindly shrub at the corner of the building and followed Gate and Alf across the bouncy planks of the porch and through the open door.

The smell of rotgut whiskey, cigar smoke, and unwashed men threatened to drown out the smells of the leather goods, a basket of lye soap, and a barrel of wrinkly apples all just inside the door. While Gate and Alf went straight through the door to the back room and the apparent source of the smells, Carson wandered around the store, fingering a bolt a gingham, and running his fingers over the steel jaws of a wolf trap. He thought of the store Ange's parents ran back in Oak Bower. A store that might have been his if things had been different. If Lijah Penne hadn't decided to rob the Oak Bower bank. If Ange were still alive.

He picked up three cans of beans and slid them under his bad arm, then he found a can of Arbuckle's Fine Coffee and carried everything toward the counter. When he set down the coffee, a tiny, old woman popped up out of her chair behind the well-worn and heavy-use-scarred wooden counter. She spit a stream of tobacco juice into the empty peach can she held in her gnarled left hand and set it on the window ledge. She gave him a toothless grin and said, "What else can I get ye?"

Carson took a deep breath and set the beans on the counter. "We could use a side of bacon and five pounds of flour and a can of lard, but first I need to know if Clifford Van Zant has been through here with his wagon train?"

The woman shook her head. "Ain't seen that rascal in a while. Not since he went north a month ago. I 'spect he'll be along one of these days. She nodded toward the door leading to the back of the building. "Y'all go on back and see Benj." She winked. "He got lots of things for you to do while you wait. I'll just put your things aside for you right on over here."

Carson found Gate at the bar nursing a glass of whiskey. Alf stood laughing and telling stories to a table full of cavalrymen in their blue uniforms.

Gate glanced up as Carson approached. "They ain't been through yet."

Carson nodded. "So I heard."

The back door opened spilling in light that was soon blocked by one of the biggest men, Carson had ever seen. The huge man lumbered in, followed by two thin, young woman wearing tight dresses and paint on their faces. The girls grinned and headed straight toward the soldiers. The big man slid in behind the bar. "Who's your friend, Gate?"

Carson held out his hand. "Carson Kettle. Pleased to meet you."

The big man's hand was surprisingly soft. "Just call me Benj. Everybody does, right Gate?"

Gate nodded.

Benj slid a glass in front of Carson and poured it full of cheap whiskey. "First one's on the house, then you gotta pay." He glanced at the girls. "You can have a tumble with either or both girls for a dollar a piece, but I expect they'll be busy for a spell. Gate says you're looking for Clifford."

Carson nodded then took a sip of the whiskey. It was all bite and harsh flavor, nothing like Mr. Grimwald's smooth bourbon or even Alf's Irish whiskey. He wiped a tear from the corner of his eye.

Benj laughed. "Got a bite, don't it?" He nodded toward the front of the trading post. "Ma puts them little hot peppers in it. Says it adds flavor."

Carson nodded toward the door. "Is that your mother

out front?" he asked, not believing such a small woman could have this huge son.

Benj roared with laughter. "Well yes and no. She's the only ma I ever knowd, but she never birthed me. Someone left me on her doorstep back in New Orleans. She took me in, and we been taking care of each other ever since."

The back door burst open, and again the light streamed in. Two dusty young cowboys burst in. The first held a half-empty bottle in his hand. The second squinted around the room and shouted, "There y'all are." He pointed to the girls, each standing behind a soldier and rubbing his shoulders.

Benj slammed a big hand on the bar, bouncing Carson's glass and making him jump. "You boy's ain't allowed in here, unless you pay up for last time and pay in advance for today. Y'all got money, come on over and have a drink. The girls are busy for a bit."

"Nope," the first cowboy said. "We just sneaked away for a little. We don't get back soon, the boss'll have our hides."

"Guess you'll have to come back tomorrow," Benj said.

The cowboy laughed and tipped back the bottle. After taking a big gulp and wiping his mustache with the sleeve of his faded, blue shirt, he passed the liquor back to his partner. As soon as the bottle left his hand, he snatched out his pistol and waved it around the room. "That don't suit us, do it, Chuck? I guess you ladies will just have to come with us, maybe spend a few days at the line camp." Carson and Gate ducked as he swung his pistol past them and toward Benj, who was easing his way down the bar. "Uh uh, big man. You just stay away from that scattergun you got under there." He glanced at his partner. "Get the girls, and let's go."

As Chuck stepped forward, the taller of the two women put her hands on her slim hips and said, "We ain't going nowhere with you two no-accounts."

For a few seconds, Carson watched, unsure of what to do. Then he slid his badge from his vest pocket and fumbled to pin it on with his left hand. He was a Deputy United States Marshal and, last he knew, Texas was still part of the United States. He moved in against Gate and eased out his pistol.

Chuck grabbed the tall girl by the arm. "Come on Honey. You too Sugar."

Honey jerked her arm free, and Carson stepped forward into Gate's outstretched arm. He was about to press through, when Gate nodded toward the door to the store part of the trading post.

The old woman pointed a long-barreled bird gun at the cowboy with his pistol out. "Time for you'uns to get back to your heifers."

The cowboy swung the pistol toward the old woman.

Flame shot from the shotgun, and gore shot from the cowboy's back. Chuck grabbed his own pistol, but before he could raise it, Alf threw his big arms around the cowboy, pinning his arms to his sides.

"Let me go," Chuck shouted. "Let go! She shot Bernie.... And we was just having a little fun."

Alf struggled to hold the wiry little man, as he twisted and fought to pull his gun hand free.

Carson darted across the rough floor. "I'm a deputy marshal. You settle down. Your friend pointed his gun at her."

Chuck stomped on Alf's foot and fought to free himself from the bear hug. "I don't give a hoot who y'all are. She shot Bernie."

Carson slammed the butt of his Colt into the struggling cowboy's jaw.

Chuck's eyes fluttered and lost focus, and, at least for the moment, his struggling stopped.

Next, Carson cracked Chuck's knuckles with the barrel of his Colt and the cowboy's heavy pistol clattered to the floor. Carson kicked it to the other side of the room.

Chuck's fluttering eyelids slowed until his eyes appeared to come back into focus. He stared at his friend, lying in a growing puddle of blood. Tears welled from his eyes. "I told you this was a bad idea, Bernie. You should have listened to me. Now look. You're shot dead."

Carson touched the young cowboy's chin with the front sight of his pistol. "You're lucky you're not dead too."

Chuck met Carson's eyes, then looked at the floor, and nodded.

"If the sergeant lets you go. I need you to promise me you'll take your friend and leave. You do anything else, anything at all, and I'll arrest you and lock you up until I can find a judge."

Chuck hung his head. "I'll leave."

Carson glanced at Gate. "Unload their pistols and give them back." When Gate picked up the two rust-pocked 1858 Remingtons, Carson turned to the soldiers still sitting around the table. "Would you men take the body outside and tie it over his saddle?" He turned back to Chuck. "Sergeant Buckley's going to let you go. Take your pistols and your friend and go home."

Gate used the point of his knife to flick the last of the brass percussion caps from the nipples of the pistols and handed the Remingtons to Chuck.

As the young man opened the door, the old lady said, "You tell Mr. Ivey, he got a problem with this to come see me."

Chuck nodded and stepped through the door.

Benj pulled three bottles from the shelf behind the bar. He glanced at the old lady, and once she nodded, set them on the bar and popped out the corks. "Drinks on the house."

Alf clapped Carson on the shoulder. "Good job, Deputy. You saved one boy's life today."

Carson nodded. "I should have done something sooner and saved them both. That Chuck's just lucky you grabbed him."

Alf laughed. "I wanted no part of Miss Berta's scattergun pointing my way, and it was all I could think of. Come on." He stepped toward the bar. "Where you going, Benj?"

Benj stopped and looked back. "You want a drink, it's all there," he said pointing to the three quickly emptying bottles on the cavalrymen's table.

Alf slapped down a five-dollar gold coin. "No offense, but we'll not be drinking that swill."

A half hour later, Carson sipped the fine whiskey Alf had paid for and watched Benj scrub the blood from the rough-hewn planks of the floor.

The old lady stepped into the room. "That's good enough, Benj. Wagons coming. We're fixin' to get busy."

4

Carson thunked down the good whiskey he'd mostly been swirling around the glass. He wanted to jump to his feet, rush out the door, and run down the road. Instead, he pushed back from the table and scratched his head. He stepped through the door, from the smoke smell of the bar, into the smells of soap and spices and coffee in the store half of the trading post and peered out the flyspecked window.

A tall man, with long white hair and a white beard, showing below a skunk-fur hat and riding a stout brown horse, led a string of wagons over the rise. As each wagon came into view, Carson scanned the horses and their drivers. And as each new wagon topped the rise and the next rumbled into view, his heart grew heavier. This must not be the right train. There must be many wagon trains taking this road to California.

Gate stepped behind him and squeezed his shoulder. "What you waiting for? Ain't this why we rode all the way from Fort Sill?"

Carson's breath quickened as he glanced back at the guide. "You mean?"

Gate nodded.

Carson stepped to the door and hesitated, his hand on the handle. What if she told him to leave her alone? What would he say? What if she said she was fine on her own, and she truly did want to go on to California, and what had she told the others in the wagon train, and what if his being here caused her problems with them? What then?

After what seemed like eternity, two big gray heads bobbed into view, one with a star and snip and the other a rapidly disappearing blaze as the horse's gray hair turned to white with age. Carson's heart thumped louder. Though he couldn't see her face in the shadow of her bonnet, he knew by her proud carriage and the turn of her shoulder it was Bella driving the team.

He took a deep breath, stepped onto the porch, and stood beside Berta and Benj. Red dust filled the air as the wagons rumbled by and began to circle on a grassy meadow between the trading post and the river.

Berta pinched his elbow. "What you waiting for? You ain't took your eyes off'a her since she topped the rise. Go on."

Carson looked at his boots. "It's not like you think. I just want to help her."

Berta spit into her peach tin. "You might fool some folks. Might even fool yourself, but you ain't fooling old Alberta Magdalene LeRoux."

Carson looked at the old woman standing beside him. "What if she doesn't feel the same way?"

"Then you got two choices. Convince her she's wrong, or slink back home with your tail twixt your legs." She gave him a little shove. "Go on. Show her how you feel."

Carson stepped from the porch, pushed past the cavalry mounts still tied to the rickety hitching rail and started up the road. He walked two steps, then broke into a run.

She looked up. A smile flashed across her face, then just as quickly disappeared.

He skidded to a stop beside her. "Bella. I.... Why...? I mean, well...."

She looked at the heavy reins in her hands, and after a moment, met his eyes. "What are you doing here?"

"I..., well..., I.... You didn't leave a note. You never said goodbye. You just left and...."

Bella looked up as the man in the skunk-fur cap rode up. "Mr. Van Zant, this is Deputy Marshal Carson Kettle."

Mr. Van Zant touched his hat. "Please to meet ya, Deputy." Then he turned to Bella. "I'll send Vern to look after your team. Once you're all settled, you buy enough vittles to keep us for two weeks. Tell Miss Berta I'll settle up with her later." He touched his hat again. "Deputy." Then he turned and galloped back to where the wagons had already formed a good part of the circle and stopped in front of the trading post, where he tipped his cap to Miss Berta and shook hands with Gate and Benj.

Bella, as beautiful as ever, sat straight and proud on the gray wood wagon seat. Carson glanced at her middle, then looked away, ashamed for even checking.

"Too early to show yet," she said, in a voice just above a whisper.

Carson's ears burned as blood rushed up his body. "I'm sorry."

She leaned over. "What have you told these folks here about me?"

He shook his head. "Nothing really." He glanced at her left hand.

She touched the gold band on her ring finger. "The people on the wagon train think I'm a new widow and that the girls are my nieces. They think I'm taking them to their father."

"Are you?"

She took a deep breath. "I pray not." A few yards before the trading post, she steered the team into their place in the circle. "Go on back to Fort Smith, Carson. There's nothing for you here."

Carson hesitated then glanced at Miss Berta on the porch. She shook her wrinkled face, then pointed toward Bella with her chin. Carson trotted a couple of steps and followed Bella's wagon until she stopped and turned the team to the outside.

He stepped in behind the closest big gray, reached down, unhooked the trace chains, and hung them on the brass hooks riveted to the hip straps.

"You don't need to do that," Bella said. "Mr. Van Zant has been sending young Vern to help us."

Carson looked around. "Don't see anyone coming." He started toward the front of the team, running his hand along the side and neck of the near horse, before passing around and unhooking the trace chains holding the off horse to the doubletree.

Gemma and her three sisters appeared from the west, scampering, laughing, and pushing one another, until Gemma looked up and smiled. "Deputy Carson. What are you doing here?"

Before Carson could say anything, Bella said, "He's just passing through on marshal business."

Carson started to explain, when Bella cleared her throat and gave him a warning look.

A gangly, blonde-headed young man of maybe twelve

or thirteen came galloping up. "I'll take them, sir. I mean, Mr. Van Zant., he's the wagon boss, he told me to come and unharness for Mrs. Foresti." He glanced from Gemma to Carson. "Them harnesses is awful heavy. I mean for a woman, not for me. I'm to take the team down to the flats by the river, then see if I can find any firewood." He glanced at Gemma and then at Bella. "Sorry I didn't get here sooner, but my ma made me take our mules down first."

Bella smiled. "Thank you, Vern." As the boy reached for the bridles, she said, "Vern Harker, this is Deputy Marshal Carson Kettle."

Vern glanced at the badge on Carson's chest. His cheeks turned red, as he nodded, "Pleased to meet you, sir. I saw Deputy Bowean Gilmour one time. He was leading three men, all trussed up. My pa told me the judge hung them three. Have you ever brung anyone in for a hanging?"

Carson thought of Lijah Penne and nodded.

Gemma stepped in and started unbuckling the quarter straps drooped between the horse's back legs.

"I'll do that," Vern said.

Gemma reached for the girth. "I'll help. And I'll help you gather the firewood."

"We'll help too," Emilia, Phillip's third daughter said.

Gemma threw her a stern look. "You three help Aunt Bella get things squared away up here."

Emilia stuck out her tongue and ran toward the river. "I bet I can find more wood than both of you." Phillip's youngest daughter, Gabriella, trotted after her sister on short, chubby legs.

Carson glanced up.

Bella's smile told of her feelings for these girls, and Carson felt something in the middle of his chest, something he hadn't felt since Ange had shared her lunch with him back in school.

Once the horses were unharnessed, and Vern and Gemma led them away down the hill, Carson said, "Can we talk?"

Something metal rattled, and Bella glanced back at Liliana pulling the cooking tripod from the wagon. "Go on and help your sisters. Lilly."

"I don't mind," Lilly said.

"Deputy Kettle can help me with things. You go on. Deputy Kettle and I need to have a grownup talk."

Lilly smiled and scampered off down the hill after Vern and her sisters.

Carson set up the tripod while Bella pulled out the heavy cast irons pots and pans and laid them out on the tailgate.

"What are you doing?" he asked.

She looked down at her pots. "You heard Mr. Van Zant. I need to go and buy supplies."

Carson pointed to the trading post, where men and women lined up out the door. "I don't think there's any hurry."

He squatted in the shade of the wagon and pointed to a stump near the blackened fire ring near the wagon.

Bella shook her head and walked over to the side of the wagon facing the store. "We'd best talk out in the open. The other women already think ill of me."

"Of you? Why"?" Carson asked.

"We'll, in their eyes, I'm an unmarried woman, who should have turned around and gone home when her husband got killed. What they don't know is, I'm a dirty liar, and I'm teaching these girls to lie too, and..." She glanced down at her middle, and tears formed in the corners of her eyes. Carson wanted to take her in his arms and comfort her, but he glanced at the trading post and saw a tall, horse-faced woman staring at them with narrowed eyes.

"Vern's mother," Bella said.

Carson couldn't help but smile and tip his hat.

Mrs. Harker looked away.

"Why did you come, Carson. I have to go away. Far away, where no one knows me."

"I don't understand."

"I have my father's books. I can teach school and raise these girls like a good widow woman. I expect God to send me to Hell for my lies, but I believe he'll forgive the girls, since they're only lying out of love for me."

Carson glanced at the porch. Mrs. Harker had disappeared into the store and no one else seemed to be paying them any mind. He touched Bella's arm. "None of this is your fault. God won't send you to Hell."

Her tear-filled eyes met his. "I wish that were true."

"Come back to Fort Smith with me. Old Mrs. Winston's been teaching at Oak Bower since my father was in school."

She pulled back her arm. "I best get those supplies ordered before there's nothing left."

Carson glanced at the trading post and saw the last of the wagon train folks go in the door. Gemma and Vern trotted up from the west laughing and dragging a huge dry branch, almost a small tree in size.

Bella started toward the store. "Maybe you and Gate could join us for supper."

"Sergeant Alf's with us too. You don't have to do that. I expect we can eat inside, or we might camp down along the river."

"Suit yourself, but I'll cook enough for everyone, and I'll

be angry if I have to throw any of it out. It's the least I can do after you rode all this way."

Carson wanted to say more. He wanted to tell her how he felt about her, but instead, he said, "Alright. "I'll help these two get a fire going, then I'll tell Gate and Alf."

Supper was a raucous affair, with Sergeant Alf and Clifford Van Zant well into their cups and full of tall tales about wars and the adventures of the trail. Bella kept the venison steaks coming and served them with potatoes and onions fried in bacon grease. As she dropped another round of steaks into the frying pan, Carson stepped behind her and reached for the fork in her hand. She jumped when his fingers brushed her wrist, and he jerked his hand back. "Let me cook those. I've eaten enough. You go eat now."

She handed him the fork and brushed a strand of black hair from her damp forehead. "Thank you," she said, "but you don't have to do that."

"Go. Get a plate. I want to."

She squeezed the back of his hand and turned away.

Van Zant laughed and said, "If'n your gonna cook those steaks, you'd best tear your eyes off the widow woman and tend to your business."

Carson pulled his eyes from Bella and turned to the skillet of venison, while Van Zant and Alf laughed. Even Gate and the girls chuckled.

As quickly as he'd started laughing, Mr. Van Zant stopped and broke into a fit of coughing.

Alf slapped him between the shoulder blades. "You all right, old man?"

Bella set her plate on the tailgate and dipped a cup of water from the bucket.

When Mr. Van Zant stopped coughing, he looked at Bella with bloodshot eyes and reached for the cup. Before he could drink, he thrust the cup back toward her and burst into another coughing fit.

Once the coughing ended, he pulled a large handkerchief from his pocket, wiped his eyes, blew his nose with a loud honk, then took the water and drank it down. "Thank you, Mrs. Foresti."

"Are you alright," Bella asked, her eyes full of concern.

Van Zant laughed. "A little meat down the wrong pipe, now where's that cobbler?"

Bella started for the Dutch oven, but Carson touched her arm and stopped her. "Could you serve it Gemma?" he asked.

Gemma jumped up at the same time Bella said, "I can get it."

Gemma already had the heavy pot and a spoon in hand. "You eat."

Bella smiled at the girl and then at Carson, picked up her plate, and sat on the ground against a wagon wheel.

A few minutes later, Mr. Van Zant swiped his sleeve over his beard and said, "Another fine meal, Mrs. Foresti." He turned toward Alf. "Now you see why I'd rather eat here than with those angry old biddies at the main fire. Speaking of which, I'd best go check on things."

"You coming back?" Alf asked.

"I'm a little weary tonight, but I might stop over yonder, later." As he walked away, another coughing fit racked his body and doubled him over. When the hacking stopped, he spit on the ground, stood straight, and walked off without looking back.

5
———

Carson lay on his back staring up at the uncountable stars of the Milky Way. Looking at the night sky always made him feel small. On one side of him, Gate gently breathed in and out. On the other side, Alf lay on top of his bedroll, still wearing his boots and britches and snoring like an angry bear.

When his father was gone to war, Carson and his mother would lie outside on a blanket, and she would teach him and then drill him on the constellations. She'd learned to find them from her father, and she loved to share her love of the night sky with him, her oldest son. Whenever a shooting star crossed the sky she always said, "Make a wish, but don't tell anyone what it is."

A bright star streaked across the sky and right over the trading post and Bella's wagon at the top of the hill. His father had come home safe and sound from the war. Maybe this wish would come true too.

As the sun pressed its first rays of light up from the eastern horizon, he rolled out of his bedroll, pulled on his boots, and wandered past their horses to the banks of the

Wichita River. He leaned against an ancient oak tree and watched the dark water flow by. He didn't know what to do, but he did know that once that sun came up and the travelers had eaten a quick breakfast, old Clifford Van Zant would wave his skunk-skin bonnet and start the wagon train toward El Paso and California beyond. He had to do something before that happened. He needed to talk to Bella one more time. Convince her to come back with him.

He turned from the river and trotted back up the hill. As he passed the trading post, someone gagged and coughed, and liquid splashed on the ground. He paused. Somebody had too much to drink. He walked on toward the wagon train. "Getting that poison out's the best thing for you," he said with a chuckle.

"Carson?" Bella said. "What..."

He turned and started toward her.

"No!" she said. "Don't come over here."

He didn't stop. "What's wrong? Are you sick?"

"I'm fine," she said, under her breath. "But keep quiet. I don't want Mr. Van Zant or the women to hear me."

"Do you need a doctor?"

She stepped close to him, the faint smell of her sickness wafting around her. "I'm fine. This is what happens to some, when...."

"I'm sorry," Carson said. "I knew that, but I didn't think."

She touched his arm and met his eyes. "You're sweet, Carson Kettle, and if things were different.... Well, I guess that doesn't matter, because they aren't."

"It matters to me."

"I've made up my mind, Carson. I'm going to California. I've got my father's books and enough money to last us until I have this baby and I can find a job teaching, and if not teaching, maybe in a store, or I could work for a doctor or something. Gemma's almost old enough, she could work and help out, and maybe someday, well someday's a long way away."

"Why won't you come back to Fort Smith with me?"

"Part of me wants to, but a bigger part tells me I need to move as far away from where those men.... From where it all happened. I don't think I could go on if I had to pass that spot in the trail again."

Still unsure of his own heart, Carson had no answer for that. He bowed his head and turned up the hill. "Come on. I'll walk you back to your wagon."

The four girls lay tangled in their blankets and with each other under the wagon. Bella glanced around then touched Carson's cheek and leaned forward and placed a soft kiss on his lips. "Goodbye, Carson Kettle." She pulled away before he could say a word and crawled back under the wagon to where she had slept.

Carson stood, his body still, but his heart and his blood racing..

"Go on, now," she said. "People will be rolling out of bed anytime now, and they already think ill of me."

His thoughts swirled as he marched down the hill. He had to do something, but what? He stopped short of their little camp and scratched his sorrel on the withers.

Almost the minute the sun reached the meadow, Gate opened his eyes and sat up. He glanced left toward Alf, still laying with his head against his saddle and rumbling like a mad bear. He looked at Carson's bedroll and then his eyes met Carson's. He pulled on his boots, stood and stretched his arms to the sky, then ambled over to where Carson stood with his horse. "Get any sleep?"

Carson shook his head. "A little I guess."

"I'm not much for advice," Gate said, "Lord knows I

usually just live day to day, but a man comes to a few big forks in the trail of his life, and no matter which fork he takes, he has to live with the choice and go on. Bella's a fine woman and she got dealt a bad hand, and even an old fool like me can see the toll it's taking on her. I see how you look at her, but you're young and taking on her burdens might be more than you can bear. Whatever you decide, you buck up and live with it." He clapped Carson on the shoulder, "I reckon we'll be heading north after breakfast." He turned away, sauntered over, and rolled Alf with his boot. "Time to go see what Miss Berta's got on the stove."

Carson wandered toward the river and turned toward the distant roar of the falls. A covey of bobwhites flushed. His heart raced. He looked over his shoulder at Gate and Alf disappearing into the back door of the trading post. He spun around and marched to his vest, hanging on an oak tree limb above his bedroll. He pulled off his badge and ran up the hill. He'd send his badge back with them and go west, no matter the consequences.

As he ran, he heard a horse splash across the ford in the river. He slowed and watched. A wild-eyed young cowboy lashed his horse with the tails of his long leather reins and drove the tired animal up the long, gentle slope to the trading post.

"Comanches!" the cowboy shouted. "Comanches!"

Carson glanced across the river but saw no sign of the Indians. He patted his hip and realized he'd left his gun belt hanging on the oak tree. He started back, then turned toward the top of the hill where the young cowboy sat on his horse and waved his hands in front of Clifford Van Zant.

He turned and let the slope of the hill carry his feet faster and faster, until he slid to a stop, strapped on his pistol, and grabbed his Yellowboy. There was still no sign of

Comanches. But he drove himself as hard as he could back up the hill.

A crowd, including Alf, Gate and the six cavalrymen, stood around the young cowboy.

Carson's still-weakened body, not ready for such a run, he stumbled.

Alf stepped from the crowd. "Slow down boyo, before you fall down. The Comanche are long gone."

Carson slowed and gasped for breath. Bella stood at the edge of the crowd, the girls huddled around her. He wanted to go to her but instead, he pinned on his badge and trotted over to the young cowboy. "I'm Deputy US Marshal Carson Kettle. What happened?"

Clifford Van Zant stepped forward. "Looks like a bunch of Comanche hit a couple of small ranches, including the one this boy came from."

"I was out at the line cabin. They killed everybody," the young cowboy said. "Took all the horses." He glanced at the woman huddled outside the circle of men. "And I can't even tell y'all what they did to those folks along the road."

"Must have been the boys who stole our mounts," Alf said. "I don't see who else it could be. Saddle up, boyos."

"I'd come with y'all," Van Zant said, "But someone's got to keep these folks here in line. Send word when it's safe to travel."

A half-hour later, Gate led Carson, Alf, and the six cavalrymen past the wagon train and toward the river.

Carson paused at Bella's wagon. "I have to go. You and the girls will be safe here with Mr. Van Zant and the other men." He looked at the four frightened girls. "Stay close to the wagon. No running off to play."

The four girls nodded.

Bella reached her hand toward him.

He touched her fingertips. "We'll get them."

She nodded and forced a smile. "Goodbye Carson Kettle. Be safe."

∽

THEY SMELLED the bodies. even before the vultures and the crows flapped and cackled into the air. Carson recognized Mr. Foresti's half-burnt wagon, the one he'd helped repair.

Between the Comanche and the birds, Phillip, lashed to the tall rear wheel he'd complained about repairing, was all but beyond recognition.

Carson pulled his bandana over his nose, to block at least some of the putrescence, and swallowed back the bitter bile that rose in his throat.

Gate remounted his bay horse and pointed west. "Come on. They went this way."

Alf and the other soldiers started their horses after the guide.

Carson dismounted.

Alf reined around. "What are you doing?"

"I won't have Bella and the girls see him like this."

Alf turned and shouted. "Jones, Brown, come back here."

The two youngest cavalrymen stopped and galloped back.

Alf pointed at the bodies. "Bury them all and drag this last wagon in behind that patch of cedars, then catch up. We'll need your rifles if we catch the devils that did this."

"Yes, Sergeant," the troopers said in unison.

"Come on, Carson," Alf said.

As they galloped to catch the others, Carson said, "I didn't like the man, but no one deserves to die like that."

Alf turned and looked Carson in the eyes. "If any man did, it was him, for leaving those sweet little girls."

They rode at a steady lope, following the tracks of at least twenty horses. A line of trees, marking a small creek wound across the prairie. A tendril of white smoke rose up past the trees and spread until it disappeared into the pale blue of the sky.

Gate stopped his horse. "Wait here. I'll go have a look." While they waited, he wound his horse ahead, staying to low ground, then dismounted and, crouching low, climbed the last rise before the creek. He stood up straight and waved them forward.

The farmer's body lay slashed and mutilated in the middle of his field of half-grown, well-weeded corn. His young wife lay naked, scalped and desecrated among broken dishes and smashed furniture on the packed red clay in front of their one-room sod house.

Gray-faced, Carson stepped from his horse and covered her mutilated body with a scrap of oilskin he found nearby. The pages of a leather-bound Bible fluttered in the breeze. He picked it up but couldn't read the German words. He turned to the pages at the front of the book and saw the names of generations of Schmidts written in several different hands. He tore the page from the Bible, folded it and tucked it into his saddlebag. With the names from the birth and death page, maybe he could contact the family and let them know what had happened, or maybe he could find a letter or something else in the soddy. He glanced up and saw Gate leaned low over his horse's shoulder, following the tracks away from the farm. "Pass me your shovel, Alf. I'll get to digging," Carson said.

Gate sat up straight, wheeled his horse around, and loped back. "No time for that. We've got to think of the living." He dismounted, grabbed the woman's feet, and dragged her toward the soddy. "They'll be just as safe in there as they would six feet under."

After another hour of riding, Gate again stopped them. He dismounted, squatted, brushed aside the grass, and touched a scattered pile of horse manure in the grass.

"What are you looking at?" Carson asked, impatient to catch up and stop the warriors. "I can see, plain as day, they carried on straight over that hill.

At first Gate frowned, pressed his lips together, and continued to crawl along the ground examining the tracks. Then he looked up at Carson. "It's not enough to know where they're going. If a man pays attention, he can tell how fast they're traveling and even if they're running scared or traveling easy."

Carson dropped his head. He had so much to learn.

"Like here," Gate said. "See how this manure's not spread out too far? They've slowed down, which tells me at least when they passed by here, an hour or two ago, they hadn't seen us."

"How can you tell it was an hour or two?" Carson asked.

"Manure's not hot, but still got a hint of warmth."

A half hour later, Gate pointed to five vultures circling. "Wait here."

Carson's heart dropped against his stomach. How many more people had to die before they stopped the young warriors?

Moments later, Gate galloped back into view and waved them forward.

The beat of galloping horses sounded behind them, and Carson reached for his rifle.

"It's alright, boyo," Alf said, "It's Jones and Brown."

Once the two cavalry men caught up, they all galloped

forward to the point where Gate had disappeared from view. Carson braced himself as he rode close enough to hear the cackling and cawing of the birds. He breathed a sigh of relief when he saw the birds feeding on the half-butchered carcass of a red mule. The animal's hide had been slit down the back and peeled back.

"Looks like they took the backstops and the tongue" Gate said. "Keep your eyes and ears open. They're going to stop soon to celebrate. We're catching up, but these youngsters must not know we're back here. We don't want to spook them. "

Gate led them away from the trail of hoof prints and wound his way in the same direction, once again keeping to low ground. The light was fading when he stopped his horse and dismounted beside a grove of scrub oak trees.

Once Carson's feet hit the ground, his mouth began to water at the faint scent of smoke and roasting meat, then he heard distant laughter. His sorrel horse looked west and pointed his ears. Carson rubbed the silky neck, until the sorrel relaxed and dropped his head for a bite of grass.

Gate gathered the men around. He turned to Alf. "Carson and I will sneak up from here. Y'all spread out to the north. Don't shoot until I do, unless you have to."

Alf nodded. "Make sure it's them."

Gate nodded. "It's them."

Alf looked from man to man. "You all saw what they did to those poor farmers. No quarter."

Grim-faced, each soldier nodded.

"We need to give them a chance to surrender," Carson said.

Alf shook his head. "As soon as they see us, they'll scatter like a nest of mice from under a lifted bundle of oats."

Carson met Alf's eyes. "After what the Grimwalds' did, it's not surprising, they went raiding."

Alf scratched his whiskered cheek, then he shook his head. "This is United States Cavalry business, Deputy Kettle. We do it my way."

Carson didn't like it, but he pressed his lips together and nodded.

As they crept forward, Carson rubbed his fingers along the smooth rawhide sleeve covering the butt of his Yellowboy. If this was how it felt to be judge, jury, and executioner, he was glad his job was to catch outlaws, not decide on their fate, unless he had no choice. Nothing was simple. If Patricia and her father had left things alone, these young men may still be living peacefully in the Territories. Yet here they all were, and as much as he hated it, he would do his duty.

6

The closer they got, the louder the young braves laughter and celebration. The smell of the roasting mule meat grew stronger and despite the tension in his body, Carson's stomach rumbled. He had eaten nothing but a biscuit and a few slabs of jerky since eating with Bella and the girls the night before.

Gate stopped and looked left and right, then he dropped to his belly and crawled to the crest of the hill.

Carson followed him and settled in behind a clump of sedge grass growing in the shade of a small oak tree.

Just before Carson drew close enough to see over the hill, Gate ducked and pressed his face against the ground.

Carson did the same.

Gate eased his head up and motioned Carson forward with his chin.

A young Comanche warrior, turkey feathers in his hair and his arms painted red, walked down the hill away from them, toward seven other young braves. One of the smiling young braves, a long blonde-haired scalp hanging from his breechclout, held up a steaming slab of roasted mule meat on a pointed stick.

Gate eased back the hammer on his Winchester. Carson did the same.

Gate's bullet took the teenage warrior walking down the hill in the middle of the back and Carson's cut through the mule meat and hit the brave, with the blonde scalp, in the middle of the chest.

The once-quiet evening air exploded with gunfire. The other six braves scattered like flushed quail. As the young Comanche scrambled for their weapons and toward the horses, Carson swung his front sight onto the next painted brave but a shot from the north dropped the youth before Carson could pull the trigger. He found another warrior sprinting toward the milling horses at the far edge of the clearing. As the young man swung onto the horse, Carson squeezed the trigger. As he levered in another round, he saw the young man lurch and heard the bullet strike flesh, then everything fell silent.

One final shot rang out. Carson raised his rifle and looked around. Gate was no longer beside him.

"I believe that's the last one," Gate shouted from the bottom of the hill, fifty or so yards to Carson's left. "Alf? You boys okay over there?"

"I think we got them all," Alf shouted back, "Take care none of them are playing possum."

They checked each body. All were dead, and most had more than one gunshot wound.

Young Cavalryman Brown pulled out his bone-handled belt knife, peeled a strip of hair from the head of the young brave with the yellow scalp in his belt, and thrust it into the air, a maniacal grin on his face.

"No," Carson shouted. "None of that."

Brown glared toward Carson, then he dropped his eyes and lowered the scalp.

"Makes us no better than them. Leave it with his body."

Brown looked to Alf.

Alf nodded his head. "Do what the deputy says and drag all these bodies off away from the fire. We might as well eat the rest of this mule meat."

Despite his earlier hunger, Carson sat alone against a large rock, his back to the others, and stared out into the darkness. He nibbled at the charred mule meat dangling from the point of his knife. Was this what his father went through in the war? One side killing a few, then the other wreaking vengeance, back and forth in an ever-bloodier cycle of death and destruction? No wonder it had taken almost a year for a flicker of the old light to return to his father's eyes after he'd come home.

Carson flicked the remains of his meat out into the darkness. Had they done the right thing, killing without warning? After what these young braves had done, he supposed any judge or jury would have sentenced them to hang. And what about Phillip? The Comanche had flayed much of the skin from his body and burned off the tip of his nose and one of his eyes from his head. Was that a just punishment for a man who would take everything and run off, leaving four beautiful daughters behind?

He shivered. Would God forgive Phillip? Say he'd already paid the price for his weakness, or was he already burning in the lake of fire and brimstone, the preacher back home always went on about?

"You alright, Boyo," Alf said walking up behind him.

Carson nodded, though he wasn't.

Alf squatted down beside him and held out another chunk of charred meat on a sharpened stick.

Carson took it. "Thank you."

"We did a good thing today. If those boys had got away. Well, you saw what they did to those people. These are hard times, and this is hard country."

"Did you fight in the war?" Carson asked.

Alf sat down. "I did."

"My father did too. Fought for the north. The whole town held it against us. He's still not the same."

"None of us are," Alf said. "At least those of us that didn't go in already murderous. And none of us will be the same after the things we saw and did today." He tapped Carson on his wounded shoulder. "You're a good man, Deputy." He rolled onto his knees and stood up. "You get some rest. I'll have the other boyos stand guard tonight."

∽

CARSON SNAPPED OPEN his eyes and reached for the pistol tucked into his blankets beside him. It was still dark. Gate squatted by the fire, blowing into a handful of tinder. As the flames licked through the twigs and grass, Carson laid back and closed his eyes. His shoulder ached and he felt as if he hadn't slept. Visions of the blonde farmer's wife, naked and mutilated, had held him sleepless until finally melding into fitful dreams of Bella and the girls.

He threw back his blanket and pulled on his boots.

Gate looked up as he approached. "Coffee'll be a few minutes. Go wake up Alf and the others."

Once they'd finished breakfast, they rounded up the horses.

Gate said, "I'll go back and let old Clifford know we got these boys." He glanced at Carson. "Unless you want to go."

Carson took a deep breath. Bella had been clear, and he still wasn't sure what he wanted. He shook his head.

They headed northeast toward the fort. At first, Carson lost himself in keeping the horses and mules gathered and trotting in a straight line. The sun climbed in the sky and a bead of sweat ran from the band of his hat and into the corner of his eye. He scrubbed at the burning with his knuckles, then started the sorrel into a lope, passing the troopers and the herd. He eased in beside Alf who led the convoy.

Alf glanced over. "Something wrong?

Carson nodded. He unpinned his badge and extended it. "Could you see this gets back to Marshal Greer?"

"What are you doing?" Alf asked.

"I guess I'm going west."

"You sure?"

Carson nodded. "I'll write the marshal a letter and explain."

Alf smiled and took the badge. "She's a fine young woman."

"I don't even know if she'll have me."

Alf's smile broadened. "I don't know much about good women, Boyo, but if I was a betting man, I'd say she will."

Carson tipped his hat and reined the sorrel south. He waved to the cavalrymen as he galloped away.

Carson alternated between trotting and loping, and he kept his head on a swivel and his eyes scanning all around for danger and ahead for Gate. He topped a rise and spotted Gate trotting up the next hill.

Gate glanced over his shoulder, then spun his horse and trotted back toward Carson.

Together, they rode until the sun was sinking in the west and the horses began to stumble. Gate eased back to a walk.

"We'll camp yonder," he said, pointing to a line of trees, marking a creek or a small river.

Carson looked south. "We should keep going. It can't be that far."

Gate stopped his bay. "We'd be riding half the night. You go on if you've a mind, but I won't do that to my horse or to my old bones. She ain't going nowhere. Old Clifford said he'd wait for us to bring word."

7

His breath rattling in his throat, Mr. Van Zant grimaced and pushed himself to his feet.

Bella looked up from where she sat in the shade of the wagon, mending a tear in Gabriella's dress. "You should rest."

"I'm fine," Mr. Van Zant said. "I don't get over there and calm things down, those Harkers will have everyone hitched and started, before we get word from the good sergeant." He pressed his hand to his chest and hobbled a few steps. Turning back, he said, "I'll be fine. Must be something I ate." He smiled. "No offense to the cook. Let's just keep this between us." He stood still for a moment, then drew back his shoulders and marched toward the group gathered around the Harker's fire.

Bella returned to her mending and promptly pricked her finger with the needle. She sucked away the drop of blood forming, poked the needle into a pinch of dress fabric, and set the garment on the back of the wagon. She watched Mr. Van Zant walk away. What would she do if something happened to him? For a moment, she wished

Carson was coming back, but she chased those thoughts away. Her burdens were her own, and after all he'd done for her, the last thing he needed was to be saddled with a ruined woman and four, no, five children that weren't his own. Besides, he'd never said he cared for her in any way other than a genuine desire to help her. Truth be told, he just felt sorry for her.

Hearing the children arguing, she spotted them on the far side of the meadow. She picked up the front of her skirt and ran toward them. "Get back here," she shouted.

The four girls looked up as one, fear in their eyes, and sprinted toward her. As they came together, Gemma glanced over her shoulder, then slowed and scooped up Gabriella, who had fallen behind with her chubby little legs. "Are they coming?"

Bella dropped to her knees and gathered all four girls into her arms. "I told you to stay close!"

Gemma again looked toward the trees.

Bella's throat closed, and tears welled in her eyes. She'd scared these sweet girls, these children who had already been through so much. She struggled to speak. "I'm sorry. They're not coming. But you need to stay close." She opened her arms and invited them to her.

Gemma hesitated, then moved in close and whispered, "We're sorry."

Vern ran up behind Bella. "Come quick, Mrs. Foresti. Something's wrong with Mr. Van Zant. My ma's tending to him but he told me to fetch you."

Bella let go of the girls and took a few sprinting steps after the gangly young man. Her head spun, and she slowed to a trot. Why had she let him go when it was obvious something was wrong with him? She should have insisted he rest.

He sat in the shade of the Harker's wagon, a cup of coffee

in his hands. He met her fear-filled eyes, then took a deep breath and looked away.

She dropped to her knees beside him.

"Just something I ate," he said.

Mrs. Harker stepped forward. "It's more than that, y'all. Look at him. His heart's going. I seen it before. Took my dear old daddy."

Mr. Van Zant grimaced, pushed himself to his feet, and cast his angry eyes on Mrs. Harker. "I'm fine, woman. It's something I ate, I tell you." He glanced toward the trading post. "Or drank."

Mr. Harker brushed by his wife. "We need to get going. With those soldiers after them, those savages are long gone. Probably hiding out in the Territories." He looked around at the other men and women. Many of them nodded at him.

Mr. Van Zant straightened his back and pulled back his shoulders. "Long as I'm in charge, we go when I say."

"And what if we don't agree?" Mr. Harker asked.

Mr. Van Zant spit a stream of tobacco juice on the ground. "Then you go on without a guide."

Mrs. Harker placed her left hand on her hip and held out her right. "We'll have our money back."

"Nope," Mr. Van Zant said. "We've got a deal. My job is to get you there safely, and that's what I'm doing. You don't like it, you go on, but there'll be no refunds." He turned to Bella. "Come on, Mrs. Foresti. Let's go make sure we've got enough bacon for the next leg."

~

BELLA, Mr. Van Zant, and the four girls ate apart from the others. Every few minutes, Mr. Van Zant took a small sip from a bottle of Miss Berta's pepper-laced whiskey.

Bella glanced at him, taking a drink.

"Don't worry. This is medicinal purposes only. Eases the pain in my chest," he said. "Just like Miss Berta told us. I'm going to buy a case before we set out." He glanced at the herd of horses grazing along the river. "You had the shoes reset on those big grays of yours?"

She lowered her eyes. How had she not thought of that? She shook her head.

"Never mind that. You've had a lot on your mind. Tomorrow we'll get Benj to fix you up. He's a fair hand with a forge and hammer."

An hour later, half the families in the wagon train huddled around the Harker's fire. The other half, at least of the men, had retired to the back room of the trading post. The murmur coming from the Harker's fire grew louder and louder until it threatened to drown out the laughter and shouting coming from the drinkers.

Mr. and Mrs. Harker and three men marched toward Bella's little fire. Mr. Harker stopped and towered over Mr. Van Zant. "We're leaving at first light. With you or without you."

Mr. Van Zant took another sip of whiskey and shrugged his shoulders.

"We took a vote," Mr. Harker said. "If you ain't coming with us, we'll have our money back."

"And we're leaving this papist harlot here," Mrs. Harker said.

Bella winced as if struck.

Mr. Van Zant's easy smile fled, and his eyes turned rock hard. He nodded, set the whiskey bottle down beside his foot, pushed on his knees with his palms, and rose. Once standing, in a blur so fast it seemed like magic, he drew his pistol, cocked it, and pressed it to Mr. Harker's forehead.

Harker's eyes opened wide, and his Adam's apple bobbed.

"Might keep that shotgun pointed at the sky, Braxton," he said. "Lessen you want to see what Harker's brains look like. As you can see, I'm already feeling better, and I already told you, go on without me if you want, but there's no refunds, and as long as I'm in charge, I'll say who is and who isn't part of this train." He turned his eyes to the other men. "You siding with this fool over me?"

Braxton and the other men looked at one another.

A black-bearded, thin man, Abraham Waldner, said. "It ain't that, really. Well, you see.... I guess we're just itching to keep moving."

"You ever seen what the Comanche do to a woman, Abe?" Mr. Van Zant asked.

Waldner shook his head.

Mr. Van Zant glanced at Bella and the girls. "I've seen it many times. You want to hear about it, we'll go across to the post and I'll fill you in."

Waldner glanced at Mr. Harker and at the other two men. "I guess we should wait. Surely it won't be more than a day or two." He turned and tipped his hat toward Bella. "No offense meant, Mrs. Foresti." He turned and walked away.

One of the other two men followed him back across the circle.

Mr. Van Zant holstered his pistol. "Wait here," he said to the Harkers. "I'll fetch your money."

Mrs. and Mr. Harker looked at each other and at Braxton. Mrs. Harker smiled. "What do you mean? I thought you said...."

Mr. Van Zant dug into his saddlebags, then stood and dropped five gold eagles into Mrs. Harker's hand. Then he held out five more coins toward Mr. Braxton.

Braxton stood with his right hand on the stock of his double-barrel shotgun and his left hand in his pocket.

"Take 'em, or don't," Mr. Van Zant said. "Won't change things either way."

Braxton took the coins with his left hand and pocketed them.

"I don't understand," Mrs. Harker said. "If the others are staying with you, we will too?"

Mr. Van Zant rested his hand on the butt of his pistol. "Ain't nothing to understand. I've changed my mind. You've got your money back, but you're the only ones. He glanced at Bella, then turned back to the Harkers. "Y'all are free to head on whenever you're ready. We'll leave as soon as we get word from Sergeant Buckley, but you won't be traveling with us."

Mr. Harker pressed his eyebrows together. "What do you mean?"

"I mean after tonight, you won't travel with us, you won't be part of the wagon circle, you won't share meals with us. You'll be on your own."

"And what if we choose to stay on?" Mr. Harker said, extending his hand, holding the coins.

Once again, like magic, the pistol appeared in Mr. Van Zant's hand. "Mutineers got no place in my train. No need to stop and say goodbye when y'all leave in the morning."

8

Carson and Gate heard the ratatatat of a farrier's hammer, before the trading post and the wagon train came into sight.

Bella's stocky grays stood tied beneath a big oak tree, switching at flies with the wispy, long hairs of their docked tails. Benj had the left foreleg, of the closest horse, tucked between his knees. His hammer flashed in the morning sun as he finished nailing a shoe to the pie-plate hoof.

Bella and Gemma stepped out of the trading post, carrying a heavy wooden crate.

"Told you, they'd wait," Gate said.

Mr. Van Zant stepped out behind them and glanced left and right. He held a double-barreled coach gun in his right hand.

Gate slid the thong from the hammer of his pistol and pushed his bay into a trot. "Come on. Something's wrong."

Carson stopped in the road in front of Bella and Gemma, stepped from his horse, and let the reins fall, ground tying him. "Let me take that," he said.

Bella kept her eyes on the crate. "We've got it, Deputy."

Carson nudged Gemma aside and lifted the entire crate, leaving Bella staring at the ground. "Where do you want me to put it?"

Bella glanced at the open tailgate of the wagon. "Set it behind the wagon. We'll clear a spot."

The bottles clinked as Carson carried them. "What's in here?"

Gemma opened her mouth, but Bella cut her off. "Medicine for Mr. Van Zant."

Carson cocked his head, but remained silent.

Behind him, Gate said, "See you're packing a scattergun, and y'all are short a wagon."

Mr. Van Zant grunted and spit on the ground. "Them Harkers and Braxton didn't want to wait for y'all to bring word."

"They went on by themselves?" Carson asked as he set the crate in the wagon.

Mr. Van Zant nodded.

"That's not safe," Carson said. He started to say something about Phillip and the others traveling with him, but he glanced at Gemma, saw fear and concern on her face, and bit his tongue.

Mr. Van Zant glanced at Bella. "Couldn't let them stay."

Bella's cheeks flushed red.

"You catch those Comanche?" Mr. Van Zant asked.

Gate nodded.

Mr. Van Zant pulled a small, flat glass bottle from a back pocket, pulled the cork, and took a small sip. "I need to sit a minute, then I'll get these folks packing. Once Benj finishes shoeing Mrs. Foresti's horses, we'll make a few miles."

Bella glanced at Benj and her horses, then picked up her heavy, black frying pan and set it in its place in the back of the wagon.

Carson glanced at Gemma, then touched Bella's arm and said, "Before you do that, I need to talk to you."

"You can talk while I work, Deputy."

"I need to talk to you in private," Carson said. He touched the pinholes in his vest. "And it's just Carson."

Bella raised an eyebrow. "What do you mean?"

Carson pointed to the porch of the trading post. "Please?"

Bella nodded. "Start packing, Gemma. I won't be long."

On the porch, Carson took off his hat and wrung it in his hands. He glanced at Gemma, then shifted until the girl couldn't see his face.

Bella looked past him at her wagon. "Say what you have to say. I already told you I'm fine on my own, and I need to pack."

"It's Phillip."

She snapped her eyes from her wagon to Carson's face. "Phillip? What about him?"

"He's gone."

"Gone?"

"Dead."

She covered her mouth with one hand, glanced at Gemma beside the wagon, and beyond her to the other three girls playing in the meadow. "You're sure?"

He nodded.

"How?"

"The Comanche."

Bella's eyes opened wide.

"I can tell the girls if you want."

She shook her head. "I'll tell them. It has to be me." She glanced down toward the ford in the Wichita River. "Vern," she said.

"Vern?" he asked.

"It's my fault," she said.

"I don't understand."

"Mr. Van Zant sent them away because of what she said about me."

"The Harkers?"

She nodded.

"What did she say?"

"It doesn't matter. I need you to go after them. Warn them. I'll get Mr. Van Zant to change his mind." She started toward the wagon, where Mr. Van Zant still sat in the shade, talking to Gate.

Carson grabbed her sleeve. "The Comanche that killed Phillip, are all dead."

"All?"

Carson looked at the ground and nodded.

Gate strode toward them. "Come on Carson. You can help me get these folks packing."

Carson looked at Bella.

She rubbed a tear from the corner of her eye. "Go on," she said. "I need to talk to the girls."

He stood a moment watching her, then turned and trotted after Gate.

The rest of the members of the wagon train stood around the big fire ring near the gap in the circle left by the Harker's departure.

Gate marched up. "Y'all get packed. We're leaving after lunch."

Carson flashed his eyes toward Gate. We? What did he mean?

Abe Waldner stepped forward. "Did you get those red devils?"

Gate nodded. "They won't bother us or anyone again."

Again, Carson looked at Gate. What did he mean by us?

"Where's Mr. Van Zant?" Abe asked.

"He's busy. He asked me to get you started packing.," Gate said, then turned away.

"He's sick," Abe said. "Mrs. Harker said it's his heart."

Gate stopped and turned back toward the gathered pioneers. "He's a tough old bird, but just in case, young Deputy Kettle and me'll be coming along."

"You? Do you know the trail?"

Gate nodded and marched off toward the trading post. "Get packed. We leave after lunch."

Carson followed him into the trading post, where Gate picked up a sack of flour and plopped it into his arms. "What do you mean we're coming? I thought you were heading back to the fort."

"Clifford's under the weather. I've been over this road a time or two. He's offered to share his pay, and I'm tired of scouting for the army."

"So, you're in charge, now?"

"Clifford and me's partners."

"Where do I fit in?"

"Clifford's going to ride with Bella. You and me are gonna keep these pilgrims safe," Gate said. He set a sack of beans on the counter.

Miss Berta stood up from her perch by the window.

"You got a good pack horse and all the tack, ma'am?" Gate asked.

"We do," she said. "You want him?"

Gate nodded. "Yes, ma'am."

"Sixty dollars. Tell Benj."

"Young Carson'll be back with the money."

Carson shot his eyes toward Gate.

Gate grinned. "Tell Clifford. He's paying. Then get the horse packed. Not too heavy, but if there's room, take a few things from Bella's wagon. Clifford's gonna be riding with her most of the time."

After lunch, Mr. Van Zant drove Bella's wagon. Bella sat on the seat beside him, and Gemma followed proudly, riding his big brown horse. He paused the team near the other wagons. "Y'all fall in line. We'll lead the way."

When they passed the freshly dug graves and the two burnt out wagons, Bella looked up at Carson.

He bowed his head, glanced toward the side of the road, and nodded. He watched, wondering how she would react. Phillip had done her nothing but wrong, but he was the children's father and he had been part of her original group of westward travelers.

She glanced over her shoulder, then moving only her wrist, crossed herself.

Carson stopped the sorrel and watched the wagons trail by, one by one, trace chains and loose items rattling, and dust puffing up at each hoof fall.

The folks riding the wagons and those walking alongside whispered to one another and stared at the charred wagon beds and the furniture and other once-loved items scattered along the road. When they passed the graves, the soldiers had dug, they fell silent, and men touched the rifles and shotguns they carried beside or behind them. The perils of the road had just become all too real.

The sun was low in the western sky when Gate galloped over a hill toward the train. Carson galloped ahead and met him as he came alongside Bella's wagon. Gate raised a hand. "There's a place to stop just ahead."

Mr. Van Zant glanced around. "David Grant's ranch, ain't much further. There's good water there."

Gate shook his head. "Not a good idea." He glanced at Bella, took a breath, and continued. "The Comanche hit them. It ain't pretty." He glanced over his shoulder. "The Harkers and Braxton saw it and they're headed back this way."

Van Zant hesitated, met Gate's eyes, then nodded. He handed the reins to Bella, stood, and waved his arm over his head. "Circle up. Leave a spot for us." he shouted. "Water from your barrels. We'll refill in the morning."

While the wagons circled the large grassy meadow, the Harker's wagon rumbled over the rise, with Braxton plodding alongside on his big dun horse.

Bella had begged Mr. Van Zant to reconsider letting Carson ride ahead and invite the Harkers back into the fold, but he had stood firm, saying they had made their own beds and now they'd have to lie in them.

"Drive on," he said. "I need to talk to Harker and Braxton." He sat back down and pulled his coach gun from behind the seat.

As they approached the two wagons, Bella eased her horses to the right side of the road.

"Hold to the middle," Mr. Van Zant said.

Mr. Harker steered his team into the grass and handed his lines to his wife. He reached into his pocket. "I've got your money right here. We'd like to rejoin you."

Mr. Van Zant shook his head. "You made your choice."

Mr. Harker glared at his wife, pale-faced and staring straight ahead, then he turned his eyes back to Mr. Van Zant. "I apologize for the way I acted. I didn't realize." He glanced over his shoulder. "There's people back there. Dead and well.... I suppose you know. All of them killed. Men, women, and children."

Mr. Van Zant held up his hand. "That's enough. Gate already told me. The rest of these women and children don't need to hear about all that."

Mr. Harker stretched out his hand. "Take it.... Please."

Mr. Van Zant shook his head. "You're not welcome back."

Gemma rode by on Mr. Van Zant's horse and stopped beside young Vern Harker, where he stood at the back corner of the wagon, kicking his toe into the dirt.

Bella squeezed Mr. Van Zant's arm and leaned close to his ear. "Please," she said. "If not for them, for their children."

Mr. Van Zant glared at Mrs. Harker. "What you got to say about this, Mrs. Harker.? You got anything to add?" He looked over at Bella.

Mrs. Harker's long face flushed deep red, and she looked over with fire in her eyes. Then she glanced over her shoulder, and the flames fled her eyes as the starch drained from her stiff shoulders and back. She looked at Mr. Van Zant. "I apologize for what I said."

"Don't apologize to me," Mr. Van Zant said.

Mrs. Harker took a deep breath. "I'm sorry for what I said, Mrs. Foresti."

Mr. Van Zant nodded. "Alright. One more chance." He took a quick sip from the bottle wedged behind the seat, climbed down from the wagon, and took the coins from Mr. Harker, then walked back and took the gold coins from Mr. Braxton.

Braxton's face remained frozen, and he held his eyes on his horse's neck.

Mr. Van Zant pocketed the coins and beckoned for Gemma to ride to him. He smiled at her and said, "thanks for looking after old Browny today, but I'll need him for a bit." Once she had slid from the saddle, he mounted and rode into the middle of the circle. "Waldner, Mc Chesney, Farnsworth, I need y'all to bring shovels and picks if you've got them. We won't be far. Just a short piece over yonder rise. The rest of you help their families get settled."

His face white, Abe Waldner stepped away from his wagon and his family and spoke quietly to Mr. Van Zant. "What is it? Should I bring my rifle?"

Mr. Van Zant nodded. "We got some burying to do. And from what Gate here says, we'll be wanting to get it done before the women and children pass by."

Carson dug the pick and shovel from Bella's wagon and galloped after the others.

He rode past the three walking men and loped toward Gate and Mr. Van Zant.

After the buzzards and the crows and the coyotes had been at the bodies, there was little recognizable as human in the yard of the Grant's ranch.

Carson spotted a bit of pink and white gingham near a patch of low brush. He trotted over, sick at heart at what he might find. As he got close, two coyotes snarled and pushed out of the brush toward him. He reached for and fumbled with his Colt.

"Move!" Mr. Van Zant shouted, and as Carson stumbled out of the way, his pistol appeared in his hand. He shot both coyotes with what sounded almost like one shot. A third coyote burst from the edge of the brush and sprinted away, a chunk of flesh and bone in its mouth.

Carson raised his pistol, but before he could draw a bead, Mr. Van Zant's bullet tumbled the fleeing animal.

It was well after dark by the time they had dug six graves, gathered and sorted the scattered remains as best they could, and buried them in a neat row beside the burned-out cabin.

Though he hadn't helped with the digging, Mr. Van

Zant's breath rattled as they rode back into view of the wagon train.

Most of the settlers stood in a circle around the Harker's fire. Carson couldn't make out the words, but he recognized Mrs. Harker's angry, grating voice above the others.

9

The light from four separate campfires flickering and dancing on the canvas coverings of the circled wagons. This night, on Carson's order, the horses milled about, confined in the center of the circle. Bella's girls and several other children chased each other from camp to camp. Bella stirred something in a pot over the small fire near her wagon. Despite the grisly task they had recently finished, Carson's mouth watered, and his stomach grumbled. He sighed. Why was Bella all alone? Many of the men and women stood around the largest of the fire rings near the Harker's wagon. Mrs. Harker's loud voice fell quiet as they topped the rise and rode into view.

Mr. Van Zant grunted and started his horse into a trot. When Gate rode up beside him and whispered a few words, he eased the horse back into a walk. As he stepped his horse over a wagon tongue and into the circle, a short, stocky, red-haired man, Mr. Corcoran, stepped forward, his lips quivering. "Wwwwwhat happened to those people? Aaaaare we safe?"

Mr. Van Zant waved a hand and squeezed his horse ahead, forcing the people to move aside or be trampled.

Mrs. Harker pushed forward. "You told us the savages had been moved to the Territories. You promised you'd keep us safe."

Mr. Van Zant stifled a cough, and his face flushed purple in the firelight. "Don't make me regret letting you rejoin, woman."

"But those poor people. You saw what they did to them."

He continued toward Bella's wagon. "Best set out a couple of guards."

Carson rode around the people gathered at the fire. "The Comanche that did this are all dead."

"How could you know that?" Mrs. Harker asked.

Carson looked toward Gate, but the tracker kept his eyes on Mr. Van Zant and followed him through the crowd.

"We killed them," Carson said. He started his horse. "Rather than jawing here around the fire, I suggest you decide who's going to take first watch and who's going to relieve them."

∼

BY THE TIME Carson finished the last of Bella's delicious stew, Mr. Van Zant lay, snoring, in his bedroll near the wagon tongue.

Abe Waldner skirted the horses and walked across the circle toward them. His wife Aggy, a rangy, big-boned woman with fair hair, and a long face, followed him, carrying a large, cloth-covered plate.

"Can we join you?" Abe asked.

When no one else answered, Carson glanced at Bella, who nodded. "Of course," he said. "Come on in."

Abe took off his hat. "Mrs. Foresti, this is my wife Aggy."

Bella smiled and nodded. "We met briefly, when I joined up."

Aggy stepped around her shorter, smaller husband and extended the plate toward Bella. "I brung you a cake."

The rich smell of cinnamon and vanilla filled the air, and though Carson had just eaten his fill, he smiled in anticipation.

Bella took the plate and smiled. "Thank you. You didn't need to do that."

Aggy nodded. "I did. I had a few eggs left from Miss Berta." She glanced toward the Harker's fire. "I shoulda done it sooner. I had a bakery back in Knoxville." She bowed her head. "I'm afraid this one's a little plainer than those I made back home."

Bella smiled and took the plate. "It smells wonderful. Let me get a knife." She came back with a long knife, cut a thin wedge of cake and placed it on a towel. She handed it to Carson. He was about to tell her to serve someone else first when she said, "Would you take this to Mr. Van Zant? One thing I've already learned is he likes his sweets."

Carson approached the snoring man and leaned close. "Mr. Van Zant."

His snoring continued unchanged.

Carson touched the older man's shoulder to shake him.

Mr. Van Zant's pistol appeared from nowhere and bumped the end of Carson's nose. Carson danced backwards, juggling the wedge of cake, and would have stumbled into the fire if Abe hadn't grabbed his sleeve.

"What?" Mr. Van Zant said.

Gate, sitting cross-legged off to one side, chuckled and said, "The deputy was just trying to give you a piece of cake. You don't want it, I'll take it."

Mr. Van Zant smiled and said, "You done a good job saving it, young man. Good thing, too. If you'd have dropped it in that fire, I'd of had to have yours."

Once everyone was served, Bella wrapped four small wedges for the children and tucked them into the wagon box. She turned to Aggy. "Thank you. It was delicious."

Aggy smiled.

Mr. Van Zant cleared his throat and asked, "What's in it? I'll buy the fixins at Fort Chadbourne if y'all'd be kind enough to bake another or two."

Aggy nodded. "I'd be pleased to." She turned toward Bella. "I'd be happy to teach you how I make it..., at least if you want."

Bella smiled. "I'd love that."

The next morning, not long after first light, they passed the remains of the Grant's ranch. As they drove past the burnt buildings and the six graves, the ever-present hum of people chattering, disappeared. They stopped at the creek just south of the ranch and filled the water barrels and watered the stock. For the rest of the morning, Carson heard nothing but the sounds of wagons thumping and bumping and creaking and trace chains rattling.

Carson brought up the rear and made sure no one fell too far behind. With a southwest wind blowing, he found himself riding in the dust stirred by the wagons. He steered the sorrel out to the west, but not before a thin layer of dust covered his hat and clothes.

An hour past the Grant's ranch, Gate rode back and stopped beside him. "Go on up and ride with Clifford. He wants to talk to you. I'll keep these stragglers moving."

Carson galloped past the wagons and reined in beside Bella's, when he saw Mr. Van Zant's brown horse trailing behind it. "You wanted to see me, sir."

Mr. Van Zant laughed. "Young Bella here has been telling me how you came to be a deputy."

Carson sat a little straighter.

"Says you brought in a wicked man by the name of Lijah Penne."

Carson nodded. "I had a lot of help," he said, trying to be humble.

Mr. Van Zant spit a stream of tobacco juice on the ground. "I've heard of Lijah Penne. Folks say he was a bad hombre."

Carson just nodded, not wanting to blow his own horn.

"And after that, Marshal Greer hired you to be a deputy?"

"Something like that, sir."

Mr. Van Zant took a sip of pepper-laced whiskey, then grinned. "Did Marshal Greer not think to teach you how to handle a pistol?"

All the boastful pride drained from Carson's body, and he slumped in the saddle. "I guess not, sir."

He glanced at Bella sitting on the seat beside the old guide. Her eyes twinkled, and she bit her lips together, but her shoulders shook with repressed laughter.

Carson puffed up. Who were they to laugh at him? He lifted the reins to ride away.

"Hold on a minute, son," Mr. Van Zant said.

Carson sat back in the saddle, and the sorrel relaxed back into stride with the big grays.

"I used to be a fair hand with a sidearm," Mr. Van Zant said.

Used to be? Carson had never seen anyone better.

"I was thinking I might teach you a thing or two. But only if you want to."

Carson grinned. "Yes sir! I'd like that a lot."

That evening, before supper, Carson looked for Bella, but she wasn't at her usual spot, stirring a pot over the fire. "Have you seen Bella," Carson asked Mr. Van Zant.

"I think she was feeling poorly. She's gone off yonder."

She appeared out of a stand of low brush, scrubbing her hands on a scrap of cloth.

Carson walked out to meet her. "Have you got a rag I could use to clean my weapons?" He stopped. Her face was pale and her eyes puffy, as if she'd been crying. "Are you alright?" he asked.

She nodded and stuffed the dirty rag in the left pocket of her dress and pulled a clean one from the right.

"You sure you're alright?"

She nodded and started back toward the wagon.

Carson stood a moment, then followed her. While she prepared their supper, he used a scrap of cotton and neatsfoot oil from a small tin to clean his Smith and Wesson pistol.

Mr. Van Zant and Gate returned from a short scouting trip they had taken to prepare for the next day.

Eager to eat and get out to shoot, Carson holstered his pistol and jumped to his feet. "I'll take your horses."

Mr. Van Zant frowned. "Load that pistol 'fore you do anything. It ain't nothing but a short club without lead in it."

Ashamed of himself, Carson looked down, pulled his pistol from the holster, broke it open, and loaded five, forty-four caliber rounds from his pocket. At first, he wanted to justify his error. He was only going to be gone for a few minutes with the horses. Instead, after hearing his father's voice in his head, he holstered the loaded pistol and said, "My mistake. I know better. It won't happen again."

After barely tasting his supper, Carson pulled a box of .44 ammunition from his saddlebags.

Mr. Van Zant pulled an extra Colt Walker from his war bag in the back of the wagon and stuck it into his gun belt. He pulled a flour sack of tin cans from the cowhide stretched under the wagon where they stored dry wood and cow chips they found along the trail. He turned toward Gate. "You coming?"

Gate looked up from his coffee and shook his head. "I carry one, but it's just for snakes and broke-legged ponies. Comes time to fight, I want to have a Winchester in my hands."

Mr. Van Zant laughed, turned, and marched a hundred yards from the wagons. He handed the sack of cans to Carson and pointed to a downed cottonwood log laying next to the little creek. "Line 'em up."

Once Carson had returned, Mr. Van Zant said, "I know I told you to keep it loaded, but now, I want you to unload it."

Carson hesitated.

"Don't want you to shoot a toe off, neither yours nor mine. Trouble comes, I'll hand you one of my Walkers," Mr. Van Zant said.

Carson patted his pocket. "I've got a little Remington two shot in here."

Mr. Van Zant nodded. "Good boy. Smart."

Carson broke the Smith and Wesson, and once again placed the cartridges in his pocket.

"Holster up and let's see ya draw, cock, and point."

Carson shoved the pistol deep into his holster and jerked it out. Even after the front sight snagged on the holster, he remembered his father's lessons. He cocked it as it came to shoulder height, and he kept the muzzle pointed away from the wagons and his finger off the trigger.

"Watch me," Mr. Van Zant said, as his Colt appeared in his hand, cocked and aimed.

Carson smiled. "How did you get so fast?"

"Practice," Mr. Van Zant said. "Nothing more and nothing less. With that easy to load pistol you've got there; you can practice any time you get a few minutes. I want you to do it ten more times right now."

The tenth draw was already much smoother than the first.

"Give me one of your cartridges," Mr. Van Zant said. As soon as Carson dropped it into his hand, Mr. Van Zant tossed it toward Carson's face.

Carson snatched it out of the air.

Mr. Van Zant grinned. "You got a good eye and quick hands. After a thousand, or ten thousand draws, you'll likely be quicker than an old man like me." He drew his pistol and shot the first five cans from the log, firing so quickly one powder explosion melted into the next. "That's just to show you," he said, pulling the loaded pistol from his belt and tucking it into his holster. "Load up and try it."

Carson loaded and faced the cans.

"One shot only. Start slow. One step at a time. Draw. Raise. Cock. Shoot. One. Two. Three. Four."

Carson pulled his pistol, raised and cocked at the same time, and fired a round into the log below the can he had aimed at.

"That's alright," Mr. Van Zant said. "That a been someone shooting at you, you'd a shot off his man parts." He chuckled. "I've seen that a time or two. Doesn't kill a fella, but it dang sure gets his attention. This time slower. I'm gonna count it out. One."

Carson drew.

"Two."

Carson raised the pistol to shoulder height.

"Three."

Carson cocked the pistol.

"Squeeze the trigger straight back. Four."

The pistol bucked, and the can flew straight back off the log.

By the time Carson had shot off half a box of ammunition, Mr. Van Zant counted at a steady pace. "One, two, three, four."

And Carson hit a can with each of his five shots.

"Good work," Mr. Van Zant said. He handed Carson the empty pistol from his belt. "Clean them both. Do you know how to load a Walker?"

Carson nodded.

"Powder and ball's in my war bag."

As they approached the circled wagons, the murmur of voices around the Harker's fire stopped.

10

Energy in the still mid-afternoon air prickled and stirred the hair on Bella's arms, and the rising humidity had her skin damp. A three-jagged-pronged fork of lightning streaked from the almost-black bottom of the huge, billowing, white cloud bank rising over the western horizon. Several seconds later, distant thunder rumbled.

Mr. Van Zant placed a hand on Bella's shoulder and used her to steady himself as he stood and looked over the wagon top at the other wagons, swaying and bouncing along behind them. He whistled and shouted. "We've got to pick up the pace if we want to get across the Brazos before that storm hits." He sat and took the lines from her. "You'd best find the girls and keep them close."

Seeing the concern in his eyes, she nodded, lifted the front of her dress with one hand, and jumped from the moving wagon.

He clucked to the team and broke them into a trot.

She glanced down the length of the wagon train. Her chest tightened. She ducked through a gap between one wagon and the next. Still no sign of the girls. She grabbed the front of her skirt and ran the length of the train.

Carson trotted along, keeping the slower wagons moving. When he looked up and saw her running, he loped ahead to meet her.

"Have you seen my girls?"

He pointed east. "Last I saw them, they were off that way."

She glanced at the storm clouds and took off running in the direction he'd pointed.

He hustled the sorrel up beside her, reached down, and pulled his left foot from the stirrup. "Climb up. We'll find them together."

She glanced at the wagons rumbling away. What would they think? She glanced once more at the clouds, took his hand, and stepped into the stirrup.

Not used to having two riders, the sorrel goosed ahead.

She threw her arms around Carson's middle to keep herself from tumbling off over the sorrel's rump.

After a few strides, the sorrel settled, and Carson pushed him into an easy lope.

She pulled herself against his strong back and craned her neck to see over his shoulder. Just being close to him calmed her. The girls would be alright. They just got distracted from their chore of gathering cow chips and dry wood.

They topped a low ridge and spotted the girls, the three Harker children, and the stocky Waldner boys running and playing in a grassy field full of wildflowers.

The children heard the horse loping toward them, stopped, and watched them approach.

"Aunt Bella!" Gabriella called, holding out a handful of pale purple flowers. "Look what I picked for you."

"What's wrong," Gemma said, as Carson stopped the horse near them.

"Big storm coming," Bella said, pointing west. "Mr. Van Zant wants us to get across the river before it hits. We've got to hurry." She slid off Carson's horse, scooped Gabriella into her arms, and kissed her cheek. "They're beautiful." She looked at the rest of the children. "Come on. Let's race."

Emilia, the second youngest of the girls, frowned. "Why are you carrying her?"

Carson stepped down and held out his arms. "Come on. You can ride old sorrel." He swung her into the saddle and the Waldner boys up behind her and rushed to catch up with Bella and the other children. "Hold on tight," he said, as the children bounced on the trotting horse. They soon caught up to Bella, Gemma, Liliana ,and Vern, who pulled his younger sister and brother by the hands.

The first gusts of cold wind hit them as the last wagon disappeared into the Brazos valley.

"Hurry!" Bella shouted, sweat streaming down her cheeks.

Gate galloped over the hill toward them. He reached for Gabriella. "Give her to me."

Bella nodded toward the Harker children, who had lagged a few paces behind. Gate reached down and swung Willy on behind his saddle. Vern lifted Sally, and Gate set her in front of himself.

Vern ducked his head and sprinted to catch up to Carson and Bella.

The first drops of cold rain hit just as they reached the crest of the long, shallow descent to the river.

Mr. Van Zant stood on the seat of Bella's wagon and waved the others past him and into the mostly shallow rocky ford.

Clouds covered the sun and wiped away the bright day. Lightning flashed. Bella counted in her head, one and two and three. Thunder cracked with enough volume to shake the earth beneath her feet.

Gabriella threw both arms around Bella's shoulders and pressed her face into the crook of her neck.

Her breath coming in gasps and her arms burning, Bella ducked her head and let the hill carry her toward the river in great stumbling strides.

As she got close to Mr. Van Zant and her wagon, Gate rode his bay into the river behind the last wagon in line.

Lightning flashed, and an instant crack of thunder hurt Bella's ears. She shuffled Gabriella to her left arm and cradled the trembling girl's head with her right hand. The skies opened and sheets of cold rain, driven by a fierce wind, drenched them.

Mr. Van Zant reached down with one hand for Gabriella. The grays whinnied and lurched ahead after the other horses. Mr. Van Zant fell to the seat, grabbed the lines with both hands, and fought the horses to a stop.

Bella splashed through the warm river water, thrust Gabriella up onto the seat, and, with trembling arms, pulled herself up beside her. She looked back and motioned for Carson and the bigger children to hurry forward.

"Go," Carson shouted. "We'll hold on to the back of the wagon."

Mr. Van Zant slapped the horses with the lines and the grays leaped against their collars and jerked the heavy wagon into the river.

Bella peaked back through the opening in the canvas over the wagon.

Vern, Gemma, and Liliana held onto the tailgate. Carson splashed through the knee-deep water, leading the sorrel.

Wide-eyed and pale, Emilia clung to the saddle horn and the Waldner boys clung to her, the saddle, and to each other.

The team reached the center of the river, and the rocky bottom fell away. The powerful animals sank low and almost went under. After a couple of powerful strokes, their necks and shoulders surged above the rushing water. The wagon, with its pitch-sealed sides, floated. The current swept it downstream, dragging the horses around until they were swimming at an angle, still pointing their noses at the other wagons and horses, now all safely on the far bank.

Bella twisted in the seat and tried to see Gemma and Liliana. The wind had torn away the tie, holding back the flap of canvas, and Bella stretched to push it aside.

The horses found footing on the river bottom and jerked the wagon around.

"My flowers!" Gabriella shouted. And then she was gone.

Bella screamed, "No!" and searched the churning water with her eyes. When Gabriella bobbed to the surface, she threw herself toward the girl, but Mr. Van Zant grabbed her collar and jerked her back.

"The boys are already going!" he shouted over the wind.

The grays leaned into their collars as the wagon wheels hit bottom and began to roll.

The purple wildflowers led Gabriella, Vern, and Carson around a bend in the river and out of sight.

∽

WITH HIS BOOTS full of water and his pistol weighing him down, Carson struggled to stay afloat, holding himself to the wagon with one hand and his horse with the other.

Bella screamed.

He let himself drift to the back of his arm and craned his neck until he could see around Vern and the wagon.

Gabriella splashed and bobbed to the surface of the river.

He thrust the reins toward Vern, but the young man had already let go of the wagon box and dog paddled away. He slammed the sorrel's reins into Gemma's hand and said, "Don't let go!"

He kicked as hard as he could with his heavy legs and pulled with his arms, using every ounce of strength he could muster.

Gabriella thrashed with her arms and fought to keep her head above the raging river.

Carson kicked harder and swam past Vern.

The boy, his face half in the water, glanced over, his eyes wide with terror.

"Don't stop!" Carson shouted over the roar of the wind and the river.

Vern renewed his paddling and pushed his chin to the surface.

The river gained speed, and Carson thought he might be able to touch bottom, but there was no time to check. He swam even harder.

Gabriella sank below the rough water.

With a mighty kick, Carson drove himself forward and caught the hem of her dress. He dragged her to him and reached for the bottom with his feet. Hitting the slick bottom, he threw the girl over his shoulder and lurched against the rushing water toward the shore.

His breath came in huge gasps as he stumbled from the water, with Gabriella hanging halfway down his back. He dropped to his knees. "Please God. Not one of the girls. Not today."

Gabriella coughed and gagged.

He pulled her forward. When she gagged again, he hung her face-down over his arm. She spewed water and the remains of her breakfast onto the wet rocks.

Bella skidded to a stop on the muddy shore, dropped to her knees, and grabbed the girl from Carson's arm.

Gabriella opened her eyes and wailed.

As the first of others ran to them, Mrs. Harker burst through. "Where's my Vern?"

Carson glanced toward the river. Barely able to make out the far shore in the pounding rain, he lurched to his feet and sprinted downstream.

He found Vern tangled in the branches of a big cottonwood sweeper. At first, he thought the boy might be moving, but it was only the rising and falling of the tree dragging his limp body up and down.

Mr. and Mrs. Harker ran up behind him. Mrs. Harker dropped to her knees and Mr. Harker hesitated, then ran toward the rushing water.

Carson launched himself and grabbed Mr. Harker by the legs and tackled him to the ground.

Mr. Harker clawed at the mud, then turned and pounded Carson's back and shoulders with both fists. "Let me go! Let me go."

Carson held on as the blows grew weaker and weaker, and Mr. Harker slumped.

"He's gone," Carson said.

Gate stopped his bay beside the two men. He pulled the rope from his saddle. "I'll go get him."

Carson pushed himself to his feet, his heart heavy. If he had done things differently, maybe Vern would still be alive. "I'll go," he said, pulling off his boots, and his gun belt and trousers. "I'm a strong swimmer." He looked up at the men and women gathered around. "You men take the rope. I'll tie him off and you can haul him in."

He took the end of the rope in his hand.

"Tie yourself off," Gate said.

He shook his head. He remembered what these sweepers and the power of the water could do, and if things shifted or the waves washed him under, he didn't want to be tangled in the rope.

The sweeper bounced up and down with each surge of the pounding and rapidly rising water, raising and lowering young Vern as if rinsing him clean..., or baptizing him.

Carson's breath caught in his throat each time the tree rose and dropped. He inched his way along the rough bark and around thick branches. By the time he reached the end, close to where Vern's body hung half under the tree, the younger bark was smooth and slick, and the trunk was only six inches around. He dropped his legs, one down each side, and locked his feet together. It was all he could do to stay upright as this thin end of the tree bounced up and down. He tied a loop in the rope and tossed it toward Vern's bobbing legs. The first throw sailed too far. He threw again, and the loop caught one leg.

He pulled back and snapped the rope tight. The giant root ball of the tree shifted, and the thin trunk bounced, and Carson spun from his perch and dropped in among the thrashing branches in the churning water. Keeping his legs locked around the trunk, he pulled on the rope until Vern's body came around and wedged against the branches and the rope came tight. Hand over aching hand, he dragged his upper body back to the tree.

With a loud crack, the trunk snapped between him and Vern, sweeping Vern past him and down the river. The rope hung in the branches along the trunk and scraped over Carson's face. He twisted and looked over his shoulder.

Vern's body, now free of the tree, bobbed face down in the quieter water on the back side of the sweeper.

He let go with his legs and let the current carry him along the rope to the lifeless body.

The men on shore hauled on the rope, but only managed to drag them back a few feet.

Carson pulled his belt knife, cut the rope and swam into a back eddy and toward shore, dragging Vern with him. When his feet found bottom, he stumbled forward and dropped to his knees. Tears of pain for Vern and his family and joy for Bella and the girls streamed down his cheeks, but no one saw them in the pounding rain.

Gate and Abe Waldner splashed out, grabbed him under the arms, and dragged him to shore, while Mr. McChesney and Mr. Farnsworth pulled Vern in and carried his body out onto the grass above the river.

Mrs. Harker fell to her knees and cradled Vern's head in her lap. She wailed and chanted over and over, "My boy.... My boy.... My sweet, sweet boy."

A bottle in one hand, and his breath wheezing in and out, Mr. Van Zant stumbled over the rocks, leaning on Bella, and Gemma. Phillip's younger daughters shuffled along behind.

Gemma took one look at Vern's body and froze. Mr. Van Zant tried to speak, but his words came out all raspy. He took a sip of the fiery whiskey and said, "Bring him back to camp, and we'll bury him proper."

Mrs. Harker turned her narrow, hate-filled eyes on him. "This is your fault! You could have waited for the storm to pass."

Mr. Harker pulled her rigid body to him and whispered in her ear.

She flashed her eyes to Bella and Gabriella. "It's all of your fault. If that foolish girl hadn't fallen from the wagon...."

Mr. Van Zant opened his mouth to speak, but broke into a coughing fit. He lifted the bottle and drank. His body convulsed with more coughing, and the whiskey sprayed from his mouth. He clutched his chest and sank to his knees.

11

The storm passed as quickly as it had come. Bright sunshine streamed down on the wagons, now circled on the banks of the Brazos, well above the high-water mark. Below them, the river raged, high and red with clay. Branches and sticks and entire trees, like the one that had trapped Vern, bobbed along in the torrent.

Mr. Van Zant lay trembling on top of his bedroll in the shadow of the wagon, out of the worst of the blazing, humid heat.

In the shade of a scrub cedar, Bella held Gemma and ran her fingers over her black hair. The other three girls leaned against them in a heap.

Beyond the Harker's wagon, three men took turns digging a grave. The red clay, flying from the now waist-deep hole, stood in sharp contrast to the green grass and the blue sky.

Mrs. Harker sat on the ground with Vern's head in her lap and stroked his fair hair. Mr. Harker, with a blank look on his face, knelt behind her, with his hands lightly against her trembling shoulders, as if he feared that to hold her any tighter would break her.

Gate stood away from the wagons, his Winchester in the crook of his arm, and glanced from the Harker's wagon to Bella's and back.

Carson didn't know what to say or do to comfort any of them, so he busied himself with cleaning and oiling his weapons. He laid his knife, his Derringer, and his Smith and Wesson out on the clean grass. He tested the edge of his knife with his thumb. Still razor sharp, he wiped the blade with the oily rag. He drizzled a little neatsfoot oil into the sheath and rubbed it into the leather with his fingers. Next, he cleaned and oiled his Derringer and finally, his Smith and Wesson and his gun belt. He buckled it on, stepped around the wagon, and practiced drawing, cocking, and aiming ten times before reloading the weapon.

Mr. Van Zant sat up and cleared his throat. "You're doing fine. Looks like they're about done digging. Call Gate for me."

Carson didn't want to yell, so he trotted over and brought Gate back.

Mr. Van Zant now stood leaning against the big rear wheel of the wagon. "Much as I hate to admit it, I think the Harker woman's right. It's been coming on for a few months, but lately it feels like someone's squeezing my heart in a vice. I feel the old devil dancing on my grave. I'm gonna need you boys to take over leading this mob."

Carson glanced up at the old man. What did he mean by 'you boys?' Gate had been over the trail, and he was a man of the wilderness. He was the perfect choice.

Gate's face turned white.

Mr. Van Zant took a small sip of whiskey and looked at

Gate. "For now, I can lay out the route, but if anything happens to me, you're the only one's been over this trail."

When Gate nodded, Carson let out the breath he'd been holding.

"And you Deputy," Mr. Van Zant said, turning to Carson. "I need you to take charge. Gate'll show you the way and give you good advice, but he's liable to start a mutiny if'n I put him in charge." He smiled at Gate. "No offense meant, old friend."

Gate met his eyes. "None taken. If you'd a asked me to take it all over, I'd a said no. Man's gotta know himself."

Carson's chest tightened. He looked from Gate to Mr. Van Zant, to Bella and the girls, and all around the wagon train. Other than Bella and all the children, he was the youngest member of the group. There was no way he could lead. He shook his head.

"I trust you can do it," Mr. Van Zant said.

"I wouldn't even know how," Carson said.

"Long as I'm here, I'll help you," Mr. Van Zant said. "Just tackle problems head on, and be fair, but firm."

Carson was about to refuse, when Mr. Van Zant said, "Don't do it for me." He glanced at Bella and the girls. "Do it for them."

Carson looked Mr. Van Zant in the eyes. "Don't tell anyone yet. Let me think on it. Maybe whatever's ailing you will pass."

Mr. Van Zant nodded. "We'd best get over there. Looks like they're getting ready to plant that good boy." He placed a hand on Gate's shoulder and started toward the Harker's wagon.

Carson stopped in front of Bella and the girls. "It's time to go over and say goodbye."

Gemma looked up with bloodshot eyes and shook her head. "I can't. They hate me. They hate all of us."

Carson reached out his hand. "Don't do it for them. Do it for Vern. He'd want you there."

∼

THEY STOOD around the grave three and four deep. The men used ropes to lower Vern's blanket-wrapped body into the ground.

Mr. McChesney read from the Bible.

"For which cause we faint not; but though our outward man perish, yet the inward man is renewed day by day.

For our light affliction, which is but for a moment, worketh for us a far more exceeding and eternal weight of glory;

While we look not at the things which are seen, but at the things which are not seen: for the things which are seen are temporal; but the things which are not seen are eternal."

He closed the book. "Young Vern's in a better place, but that doesn't lessen the pain in the hearts of his mother and father and brother and sister, or in all of us. Does anyone else have anything to say?" He looked at Mr. and Mrs. Harker, but neither looked up.

When no one else spoke up, Carson took a step forward. "I didn't know him long, but Vern was as fine a young man as I've met. He was always smiling and kind to everyone, and he never shirked a task. I'll miss him." He stepped back and lowered his head, as several in the group said 'Amen.' Why had he spoken? It wasn't like him, but it felt like something more needed to be said to commemorate a life taken so young.

Mr. Harker glanced up at him and nodded.

THE MEN DROPPED the last shovelful of dirt on the grave and tamped it down.

Mr. Van Zant clapped a hand on Carson's shoulder and squeezed before turning to the crowd. "We'll leave at first light, but while you're all here, I've got something to say." He looked around the group. "I'm feeling poorly and I'm afeard Mrs. Harker's right about my heart. From here on, ol' Gate will chart the path and call for start and stop times, and Deputy Kettle here'll be my eyes and ears and mouth. If he gives an order, take it as if it come from me."

Carson snapped his head around and glared at the old man. He hadn't agreed to this.

The settlers leaned together and began to whisper to one another.

Mr. Corcoran, his face bright red, said, "He's not a deputy anymore, and he's barely old enough to shave."

Mr. Van Zant took a sip from his bottle. "He brought in Lijah Penne, and I've watched him since he joined us. He's the man for the job, and I'll be guiding him."

Carson didn't notice anything around himself as they walked back to Bella's wagon. He wasn't ready to lead a group like this. Prior to going after Lijah Penne, he'd never traveled farther than Fort Smith, and he had certainly never given orders to older, more experienced men. Maybe Mr. Van Zant would recover. At very least, as long as he was there with the wagon train, he would make the decisions and Carson would only have to carry out his orders.

After picking at his supper, he walked down to the river and watched the debris bob by. Soft footsteps padded down the trail behind him.

Bella stopped close enough to his side that he smelled

the flower-scented soap she washed with. "Are you alright?" she asked.

"He said he'd wait and let me decide. At least, I asked him to wait, and he didn't say no."

She brushed her fingertips over the back of his hand. "He made the right choice."

"Maybe he'll get better."

"He's dying," she said, almost under her breath. "And he knows it."

"Why didn't he leave Harker in charge? He thinks he knows everything."

"That's why." She touched his cheek and drew his eyes. "Thank you for convincing Gemma to see Vern off."

"How is she?"

"She's sad. She's had so much loss for one so young."

He nodded. "It doesn't seem fair."

She lowered her eyes. "It doesn't, and I still haven't told her about Phillip."

"Do you want me to? I should have told them as soon as I got back."

She looked out at the river, then took his hand. "Let's tell them together."

∾

ONCE THEY'D TOLD the children about their father, Bella wrapped them in her blankets and her love.

Carson stared out into the night and drew and cocked his pistol again and again and, keeping his finger off the trigger, pointed it out into the dark at the silhouette of a baby pine tree.

What would happen in the morning? Would the others be ready to travel at first light? Would they even listen to him if he gave an order? And if they didn't, what would he do?

~

AFTER A NIGHT of tossing and turning, Carson watched the first wedge of light push up from the eastern horizon. He rolled from his blankets, rubbed his eyes, and climbed to his feet.

Gate sat on the wagon tongue, sipping on a cup of pungent, last-night's coffee. "I'll get Bella started on breakfast."

"I'm awake," she whispered.

Carson turned back to Gate. "You going to get them moving?"

Gate shook his head, and even in the dim light, Carson saw the twinkle in his eye. He glanced at Mr. Van Zant softly snoring in his blankets. "Looks like he's leaving that to you. You might as well get started today."

This was the first time Carson had crawled out of his bedroll before Mr. Van Zant. Maybe folks were already up and about. They knew they were leaving at first light. He scanned the camp. No one stirred. He strapped on his pistol and started across the circle, straight to the Harker's wagon.

Mr. Harker sat on the tongue of his wagon and stared into the darkness toward Vern's grave.

"Once I get everyone moving, I'll come back and help you with your team," Carson said.

Mr. Harker pointed toward the grave with his chin. "She says we're not leaving today."

Carson's heart sank. This was exactly what he'd feared. "You need to convince her."

Mr. Harker shook his head. "I don't have it in me. I guess it's your job now."

Carson didn't know what to say. He took a deep breath and stepped over the wagon tongue. "I'll talk to her. Get your children up and take them over to Mrs. Foresti's wagon for breakfast. Tell her I sent you."

Mr. Harker looked at his children sleeping under the wagon, and he nodded. "They went to bed with a few dry biscuits for supper."

Carson found Mrs. Harker lying on the fresh-dug dirt, a wool blanket tossed over her. "Your husband's going to take the children across to Mrs. Foresti's wagon for breakfast."

She stared straight ahead, as if she hadn't heard.

"You should join them. We're leaving as soon as everyone's eaten."

Still, she refused to look at him.

"Please. I know how hard it must be."

She turned her eyes on him. "You know? You know? You know nothing. Who have you lost?"

He started to tell her about Ange, but instead said, "I can't begin to imagine what it must be like to lose a fine son like Vern, but we have to go on, so please get up and help your husband get ready. It's not safe to travel alone."

She turned her eyes away and slumped deeper onto the dirty ground.

"I need to get everyone up. Come to Mrs. Foresti's wagon." He stood a moment, then turned and went about waking the other members of the wagon train. When he made it back to Bella's wagon, he found Sally and Willy Harker and Bella's girls shoveling in oatmeal porridge. The smell of molasses hit his nose, and the brown stains around the children's faces showed they'd all had a good dollop.

Mr. Harker stood with his back to the fire, staring across

at his wife, still lying on his son's grave. He shook his head. "I ain't hungry."

"Let's go harness your horses and pack your things."

"I suppose," Mr. Harker said, "but we won't be leaving with y'all."

Once all the wagons were loaded and the teams hitched, Carson walked over to Vern's grave, where Mr. Harker pleaded with his wife.

As he got close, she picked up a handful of clay and flung it at him. Her blood-reddened eyes raged. "You could have saved him. It was the girl's fault. She's the one he went after, yet you chose her and left my boy to drown." She turned her face away. "I won't leave him alone in this cold dirt. You take your papist harlot and her ill got brood and go on. We'uns and our friends gonna stay right here with Vern."

Blood coursed through Carson's body. How dare she talk about Bella like that? Bella had done nothing to offend this woman. He bit back his anger. He would deal with this later. Right now, he had to act like a leader. He turned to Mr. Harker. "Get your children in the wagon. I'll be right back."

Moments later, he returned with Mr. McChesney and Mr. Corcoran. "I'm so sorry ma'am, but I won't leave you here." He looked at Mr. Harker, who nodded, then he grabbed Mrs. Harker's right arm.

She slashed the fingernails of her other hand across his face and kicked out with both legs.

He dropped onto her and wrapped his arms around both of hers, pressing them against her body. "Grab her legs! She can't stay here."

McChesney and Corcoran each grabbed an ankle and together they picked up the thrashing woman and carried her toward her family's wagon.

From the back of the wagon, Sally and Willy watched, wide-eyed, as the men carried their mother toward them.

Carson leaned in and said, "Sally and Willy are watching."

Her struggles lessened, but she still twisted and tossed her head.

"Don't make me hogtie you in front of them. They've already lost their brother."

Her thrashing stopped, and she burst into heart-wrenching sobs.

Carson waved at Gate and pointed down the trail.

Gate whistled and started the wagons southwest.

Carson met Mr. Harker's eyes. "Do you want me to ride with you?"

Mr. Harker stepped close to his wife and caressed her cheek. "Do I need the deputy, Eva?"

She shook her head.

Carson nodded, and the men holding her legs, set her feet on the ground. He helped her up onto the wagon seat.

Bella drove her wagon past them with Carson's sorrel and his packhorse and Mr. Van Zant's horse tied to the back of the wagon. Carson looked all around for Mr. Van Zant, but he was nowhere to be seen.

They stopped at midday to rest the horses. One by one, the men unhitched and drove their teams to the small stream, running from a spring, bubbling from the ground, and let them drink.

Mr. Van Zant crawled from his pallet in the back of Bella's wagon. He stepped to the ground and grabbed the wagon to steady himself. His shallow breaths rattled in and out. With squinting, red eyes, he watched Carson approach. "Glad to see you got them moving. I knew you could do it."

Carson smiled and nodded toward the Harker's wagon. "Wasn't easy."

"She's a tough nut to crack, but at least you got her. Bella told me you had to wrestle her into the wagon. Might have been easier to leave her behind."

"I couldn't do that to her or her family. Not after losing Vern."

Mr. Van Zant nodded. "Hope you don't live to regret that."

12

While Carson watered the horses, Bella dug cold biscuits and bacon from the wagon, and Gemma brought a bucket of fresh water from the spring. The water tasted a little salty, but on a hot day, it was better than the tepid water in the barrels lashed to the wagon. Carson took a second dipper full and poured its cool contents over his head and neck.

∼

By late afternoon, the blazing sun had drained the spring from the horses' step and the starch from the people's backs. Even the children, usually running and playing, plodded along in the shade of the covered wagons.

Gate rode back from the south and stopped beside Carson and leaned close. "There's a bunch of Buffalo hunters got their hide wagons parked beside the river on either side of the road up ahead. They're a rough crew. We can cut west here. It'll be three or four extra miles, but there's a good big meadow where we can stop and a decent ford where we can cross."

Carson glanced back at the horses and the people of the wagon train. "Is there enough grass for us and them if we stick to the road?"

Gate nodded. "Plenty."

Carson motioned toward the wagons. "I don't know they can go an extra three or four miles today."

~

THE MEATY, gamey smell of dried buffalo hides, and the men who hauled them, drifted on the wind long before they drove the wagons into sight of the hunters.

Carson led the wagon train west of where the six buffalo hunters' wagons, each piled close to ten feet high with dried hides, sat above the river in a loose circle.

Behind him, Mr. Corcoran shouted. "Hey! Why are you stopping?"

Bella had stopped her wagon in the middle of the road. She stared at the buffalo hunters, now gathered at the edge of their wagons, watching the settlers drive their teams west.

Carson waved Mr. McChesney, driving the lead wagon forward. "Pick a good flat spot above the high-water line." Then he galloped back to where Bella still sat staring at the dirty, heavy-bearded, grime-covered hunters. "What's wrong?"

She glanced at him, then right back at the hunters and laid her hand on her belly.

Carson took hold of the cheekpiece of the bridle on the closest gray horse and led the team to the side of the road. He waved Mr. Corcoran on, then turned to Bella. "We'll be safe. I'll set out guards."

Bella looked past him and shouted, "Gemma! Bring your sisters."

Mr. Van Zant pushed his head through the wagon cover. Sweat pasted his hair to his head and drizzled down his cheeks. "What is it?" He asked, his pistol in his hand. He squinted. "Baldy Paterson and his boys."

"You know them?" Carson asked.

Mr. Van Zant nodded.

"Will they be any trouble?"

"They're a rough crew, but long as they've already drank up all their whiskey, they'll be fine."

Gemma ran up alongside the wagon, dragging Gabriella and Emilia; Liliana ran close on her heels. "What's wrong?"

"Stay with the wagon!" Bella said.

Mr. Van Zant looked from Bella to Carson, then said, "Let me get down. I'll go have a word with Baldy."

By the time Mr. Van Zant crawled from the wagon and took ten steps, he had to stop and catch his breath.

Carson stepped from his saddle and handed the sorrel's reins to Mr. Van Zant. "Take my horse. I'll ride with Bella." As Mr. Van Zant mounted and rode toward the hunter's camp, Carson climbed onto the seat of Bella's wagon, took the driving lines, and started the team after the other wagons, already circling on a flat, grassy meadow above the river.

Bella glanced at the buffalo hunters, then turned to the girls. "You stay in the circle."

Gemma looked up. "What about firewood and water?"

"We'll make do with what we've got on the wagon."

"Why?" Gemma asked.

Carson placed a hand on Bella's wrist. "One of us can go with the girls to gather some wood and water, and when Mr. Van Zant comes back. He can keep an eye on them too."

Bella, eyes locked on the buffalo hunters, nodded.

"Come on Gemma. Let's get unhitched and water these horses. You other girls can come too, if you want. We'll see if we can find some dry wood along the river." Again, he laid a hand on Bella's wrist. "I won't let them out of my sight."

By the time they reached the river with the team of grays, Mr. Van Zant's horse, and Carson's packhorse, Mr. Van Zant rode up on Carson's sorrel and let him drop his nose into the river and suck in the muddy water. "Just what I thought," he said. "They're on their way to town to sell those hides, but they're long out of whiskey. Fact, they asked me if'n we had any." He chuckled, then broke into a coughing fit.

After supper, Bella hovered over the girls like a mother hen. Fed and rested, the girls chaffed at the restriction and begged to go play with the other children. Bella just shook her head and said, "not tonight." And though she refused to explain why to the girls, Carson understood what drove her fear.

Wanting to go check on the rest of the wagon train, he turned to ask Mr. Van Zant to keep an eye on things. Mr. Van Zant sat leaned against a wagon wheel, his coffee cup hanging from a finger, his eyes closed, and his rhythmic breath rattling in and out.

Carson stepped around the wagon, out of sight of the others, and took twenty practice draws.

Gate, purpose in his stride, walked from the buffalo hunters' camp. "I think you'd better get down there. Corcoran just offered to trade a gallon of corn whiskey for a fancy Indian knife one of those boys has got."

Carson glanced at the hunters' camp. Corcoran stood laughing and talking to the rough men. He turned to Gate and leaned close. "Bella's worried. Can you keep an eye her, while I go have a talk with Corcoran?"

Gate nodded, and Carson trotted across the meadow. He met Corcoran coming back to camp, a large knife, almost a sword, with a beaded grip in his hand.

"I hope you didn't trade a jug of whiskey for that?" Carson said.

"I wish," Corcoran replied, shaking his head and grinning. "He drove a hard bargain. I had to give him two. But look at this knife." He held the knife out, beaded grip first.

Carson ignored it. "Did you already give it to them?"

Corcoran nodded. "Wouldn't have the knife if I hadn't. Why?"

"Gate and Mr. Van Zant say they're a rough crew. Rougher when they've been drinking."

"Hadn't thought of that. I just saw the knife, and whiskey's the only thing they wanted."

As the evening turned to night, the laughter and singing from the hunters' camp grew louder and louder.

Carson considered going over and asking them to quiet down, but suspected it would do him no good. So he poured a cup of coffee and set himself on the far side of the wagon to watch.

The hunters built up their fire until flames rose almost as high as the hides piled on their wagons.

"Wilma," Mrs. McChesney called. "Luther?" A few minutes later, she called out again. "Has anyone seen my Wilma?"

Carson listened, hoping Wilma or Luther would speak up. He peered over at the hunters, praying the girl was not with them.

Mrs. McChesney ran up to Bella's fire. "Where's the deputy? My Wilma went down to the river, and she hasn't come back. Luther went to find her, and he hasn't come back either."

Carson stepped around the wagon. "How long have they been gone?"

"Wilma, maybe half an hour. Luther, just a few minutes. We were cleaning up and thought she'd likely stopped off to visit with somebody." She glanced past the wagon at the hunters' blazing fire. "You don't think...?" She started forward.

Carson grabbed her shoulder and stopped her. "I'll go check."

Bella turned to Carson, her eyes filled with fear.

"I'll come with you," Gate said.

"I want you to stay here with Bella and the girls," Carson said.

Mr. Van Zant pushed himself to his feet. "I'll stand guard here. Gemma, my dear, fetch my old coach gun."

Carson and Gate trotted across the meadow. "I don't see either of them," Gate said, "but four of the boys are missing. There were twelve of them when I was here earlier."

Carson loosened his pistol in his holster and stepped into the firelight.

Mr. Braxton, a tin coffee cup in his hand, looked up from across the hunters' fire and nodded.

Baldy Paterson, a bear of a man with a fringe of greasy salt and pepper hair and a chest-length, unkempt beard, held up a jug. "If you come to drink, I hope you brought your own." He laughed, raised the jug to his lips, then lowered it and turned it upside down to show he'd emptied it.

"We're looking for a young lady."

Baldy laughed. "You ain't likely to find one here," he

said, gesturing toward the filthy men around the fire. "But if you find one, bring her over when you're done."

The men laughed and slapped their knees.

Gate stepped forward. "Where's the rest of your crew?"

Baldy looked around. "Them Whatleys ain't really with us. Just tagging along." He pointed to two wagons off to one side. "Them mangy hides belongs to them." He turned to the other men. "Where'd the Whatleys get to?"

The men glanced at one another and shrugged. A thin red-haired man with no front teeth said, "Dave come up and called 'em away. Don't know where they went."

Carson's chest tightened. "Which way did they go?"

The man nodded toward the river.

Gate and Carson turned and trotted off into the darkness.

Gate grabbed Carson's arm and stopped him.

Carson jerked free and was about to run on when Gate held a hand to his ear.

Further downstream, a muffled woman's sobs sounded over the breeze in the trees and the bubbling of the river.

Hurrying, but now careful to be quiet, Carson led the way toward the sound.

The four Whatley brothers had Wilma McChesney in a small moonlit clearing along the river. She had a filthy scrap of cloth tied through her mouth. One brother watched, while two held Wilma's arms and the fourth caressed her cheek. He grinned and said, "Look at her trembling like a little dove."

Carson stepped into the moonlit clearing. "You boys have had your fun, now let her go."

The tall man standing and watching stepped forward. "Git on outta here. We catched her. She's ours."

"I said let her go."

"I said, git!"

Wilma met Carson's quick glance with fear-filled eyes. Her face was dirty, and her dress torn away from one shoulder, but other than that, she appeared unharmed.

Carson took another step forward. "She's coming back with us. Her mother's worried about her."

The tall man laughed. "Send her mamma on down here to git her."

"Just let her go and we'll forget this even happened."

"Do you know who you're talking to, boy?"

Carson shook his head. "It doesn't matter. We're taking her with us."

The man stuck his left thumb in one of his braces and looked at the others. "He don't know who I am." He chuckled. "Should I tell him, or just kill him, Jeffrey?"

The three men surrounding Wilma laughed. The one who had caressed her cheek, a shorter version of the tall man, said, "Best tell him. Give him a chance to tuck his tail and skedaddle. It's not like we want to keep her forever. We'll send her back to her mamma come daylight."

The tall man stepped forward. "Name's Ike Whatley. I've killed near thirty men and boys. Most saltier than y'all, and that don't count Injuns and darkies."

Carson remembered a poster on Ike Whatley. The man in the poster was clean shaven and supposed to be a sharp dresser, but add a beard and filthy clothes, and this could be him. Carson's hands trembled. Ike Whatley and his brothers were wanted for murdering a stagecoach driver, the guard riding shotgun, and all the passengers, including two young women they had taken and defiled before cutting their throats and leaving them on the trail as a warning to the town marshal and his posse. There was a substantial reward offered by the young women's mine-owning father.

Ike stepped forward. "I think I'll just kill them both," he said as he reached for his pistol.

Ike's gun barked just as Carson got his pistol lined up. The bullet slammed into the dirt near Carson's feet.

Carson's Smith and Wesson jerked in his hand and his bullet took Ike in the middle of the chest. Keeping his pistol raised, Carson dropped into a crouch and scrambled to his left.

Gate's rifle barked again and again, but Carson's eyes were locked on Jeffery Whatley, whose first shot had cut the air Carson had just left, and who's smoking pistol was moving his way.

Carson shot as he dove to the ground and rolled. His first shot hit Jeffrey in the shoulder and his second in the belly.

The night fell silent.

Jeffrey looked down at the blood blossoming on his filthy, buffalo-blood-and-fat-stained shirt. His pistol hung from his fingers. "I'm gut shot, Ike." He looked up at Carson. "You gut shot me." He raised the pistol.

Carson shot him in the head.

Wilma ran and threw her arms around Carson. She tried to speak around the gag.

Carson glanced around. The other two Whatley brothers lay on the ground near where they had held Wilma, and Gate stood to one side, thumbing rounds into his Winchester. Carson holstered his pistol and pushed Wilma back enough to look her in the eye. "They're all dead. Let's get that rag out of your mouth and get you home."

At the sound of running men, Carson dragged Wilma in behind an old oak tree. He opened his pistol, dumped the spent brass on the ground and thumbed in fresh shells from his belt.

"Ike?" Baldy shouted. "Gate? What's going on over here."

"Go back to your fire, Baldy," Gate shouted.

"You kill Ike and the boys?" Baldy asked.

"I'm Deputy United States Marshal Carson Kettle," Carson shouted, wondering if Marty had already handed in his badge. "These men were all wanted, and they were planning evil on a young woman from the wagon train. Go on back to your fire."

"Who else you looking for?" Baldy asked.

"Nobody," Carson said. "Just these four. Go on back to your fire and we'll leave it at that."

After some unintelligible whispering, Baldy shouted, "We're going back. We'll be gone at first light. Can we take those boy's hides?"

"Did they have saddle horses?" Carson asked.

"Yep," Baldy replied, "and mules for the wagons."

"You boys bring over their horses. We'll need them to pack the bodies in. Take whatever of the rest you want," Carson said. "They won't be needing it."

Someone crashed through the trees behind them. Carson pushed Wilma behind him and raised his pistol.

"Wilma?" Mr. McChesney shouted. "Wilma!"

"I'm here Papa," Wilma replied. She brushed by Carson and ran into her father's arms.

Her father embraced her. "You hurt?"

"Nope. At least not much. Carson saved me."

13

The sun had been up for half an hour as Carson hoisted the four stiff bodies onto their horses and lashed them hand to foot and around their waist to the horns on their saddles. A flea crawled from Ike Whatley's hair and hopped onto Carson's sleeve. He pinched it between his thumb and forefinger and wiped the dot of blood onto his pant leg. Then he scratched his own head and neck.

The stench of dried blood and rancid buffalo fat tickled his nose. How did men let themselves get so foul? He supposed it was a matter of necessity when your day-to-day job was skinning buffalo out on the prairie. At one time, he'd considered riding west to shoot buffalo. He'd heard a man good with a rifle could earn a stake, and he had a fine Sharps.

Now he was glad he'd taken the deputy job. But like the dream of hunting shaggies for fame and fortune, that was gone too.

He hurried down to the buffalo hunters' camp before first light and had Baldy Paterson sign an affidavit swearing that he knew these men were the Whatley brothers.

With the affidavit and the wanted poster tucked in his saddlebag with the other posters he still carried there, he tightened the cinch on the sorrel. People were watering horses and starting fires back at the camp. Maybe he should stop for breakfast, but no, he's already told them he would be leaving first thing. For a moment, his heart tightened until soft footsteps and the faint scent of lavender reached him.

The morning sun sparkling off her dark hair, created a halo around her head, as if she were an angel.

"Are you sure you have to go right now?" she asked. "You could just ride with the rest of us. We'll get there soon enough."

"I'd best get there quick as I can, in case the law there needs to identify these bodies. They won't last long in this heat. These men killed a man's daughters and some other people. That father will want to know for sure they're dead."

"Won't bring back his daughters."

Carson took a deep breath before replying. "No, but he can quit looking for their killers, and he may take some comfort in knowing they're burning in Hell."

"Do you believe in Hell, Carson?" she asked, looking into his eyes.

"There's got to be a place for men like these and those that...." He bit off his words.

She looked at the ground. "I wonder if I'm going to Hell."

He stepped closer. "Why would you say that?"

"I've prayed that the poor child growing in me would be taken and it was."

Carson glanced down at her middle.

"God or the devil took it out of me. What kind of mother

could pray for the death of a child growing inside of her?" Tears welled in her eyes and rolled down her cheeks.

Carson gently touched her cheeks and brushed the tears away. Not caring who might see, he took her in his arms. The clean smell of her hair filled his head. "You're not going to Hell. You're the finest woman I know, and the strongest. That baby's life was in God's hands, not yours."

"I don't want you to go," she said. "I'm afraid."

"Gate and Mr. Van Zant will look after you. They know more about this country than just about anyone."

"Are you sure you have to go?"

He nodded. "I want to get these bodies to Fort Concho before they start stinking any more than they already do, and I need to send a letter to Marshal Greer and see if I can collect the reward money or at least get it started on its way. I'll wait for you there." He reached into his pocket and pulled out his little Derringer. "I want you to have this. Keep it with you. Do you know how to shoot it?"

She nodded, took the pistol, and dropped it into her dress pocket. Then she leaned in and planted a soft, quick kiss on his cheek, and turned and ran back to her wagon.

He stood a moment and watched her, then mounted the sorrel. As he started toward Fort Concho, Mr. Van Zant's coughing stopped him.

Mr. Van Zant waved Bella back toward the wagons and held up a hand to stop Carson.

Bella hesitated, but Mr. Van Zant said something to her, and she walked away.

Mr. Van Zant probably needed something brought back from Fort Concho, so Carson led the horses back to the old man.

Mr. Van Zant cleared his phlegmy throat. "Anything happens to me..." He cleared his throat again. "I ain't lived a frugal life. All I own's with me now, and mostly it's the money these pilgrims paid for this trip."

Carson nodded. "Nothing's going to happen to you but tell me where to send the money and I'll make sure it gets there."

Mr. Van Zant shook his head. "I got nobody left. I want you to see that Bella and the girls get it."

"Does she know?"

Mr. Van Zant nodded.

∼

CARSON RODE WELL into the night and half the next day. He followed the road across a dry prairie, dotted with scrub cedar and thorny brush, keeping the winding line of gray-trunked, leafy-green cottonwoods and thick, darker green brush of the Concho River on his left.

Cattle dotted the draws rising from the river, and he passed a set of ranch buildings built on a bank above the Concho. A little further on, he passed three farms, the third near where the north fork of the Concho met the branch he followed. The road forked before the confluence. One branch ran southwest across the north fork toward a cluster of rough buildings. The other branch turned south into a ford in the river, and beyond it, to several low, neat, stone buildings. Behind the buildings, a dozen soldiers in blue uniforms marched in the hot afternoon sun.

He looked around for a stockade or a gate like they had at Fort Sill, but saw nothing. He glanced once more at the rough buildings to the west, then rode into the river and across. Surely the marching soldiers would point him to the fort.

Halfway across the open area between the river and the

stone buildings stood a thin, narrow adobe structure. Two soldiers stepped out of the adobe, and one of them held up a hand and said, "State your business."

Carson glanced from one soldier to the other. "I'm looking for Fort Concho."

The soldiers both stared at the corpses lashed to the horses trailing Carson. The same soldier said, "You've found it. Now state your business."

"I've got these wanted men, and I'd like to see the commanding officer."

"Major Bilgely's not inclined to meet with bounty hunters, but Deputy Kerr just rode in last night. You may want to see him. State your name."

"I'm Deputy US Marshal Carson Kettle, well, er, I was." Carson's sweating cheeks got even hotter. "It's complicated. But I would like to see Deputy Kerr."

The soldiers looked at one another, then back at Carson. "Show us your badge and you can ride on in."

"Well, that's the part that's complicated," Carson said. "I don't have it."

"Step down and move those bodies downwind, and you can wait in the shade."

The other soldier trotted away toward the stone buildings.

"Private George Wright," the soldier said, offering his hand.

"Carson Kettle."

Private Wright waved his hand in front of his face. "How long they been dead?"

Carson glanced back at the fly-covered heads of the stinking corpses. "Only a couple of days, but they didn't smell too good when they were alive. Buffalo skinners."

Private Wright nodded.

The second private returned along the dusty trail from the buildings. A tall, dark-haired man, with a gray-tipped mustache, shaped like an upside-down U, and a tarnished and dented United States Deputy Marshal's badge on his shirt, walked in stride with the private. The deputy glanced at the corpses and held out his hand. "John Kerr."

"Carson Kettle."

"Where you from, Deputy?" Kerr asked.

"Fort Smith," Carson said.

"Fort Smith?" He smiled. "I started up there chasing bandits in the Territories with Marshal Greer. How is the old reprobate?"

"Fine, I guess, but, well, what I should tell you is that I resigned from the Marshals, but I'm having second thoughts, and I don't know if my partner's even told Marshal Greer, and I've been thinking the whole way down here and maybe..."

Kerr laughed and held up a hand. "Hold on, son. Let's get these bodies and ourselves out of the sun and you can tell me all about it."

They unloaded the bodies and laid them out in the shade of a porch roof on the flat-stone entry to one of the long stone buildings.

Carson dug the wanted poster and the affidavits he had made Baldy Paterson and Gate sign.

Deputy Kerr looked at the poster, featuring Ike Whatley's picture and mentioning his three brothers. "Which one's Ike?"

Carson pushed on the tallest corpse with the toe of his boot. Flies rose and buzzed from the swollen face.

"Hard to tell, with those whiskers."

"They had a young woman from the wagon train, and he

tried to warn me off by saying he was Ike Whatley. Gate heard him too."

"I know Gate, He's rock solid."

Carson nodded. "He'll be along in a couple of days with the wagon train."

"Poster shows a scar on his lip," Deputy Kerr said. He pulled his belt knife and carefully shaved away enough of the hair to see the mottled skin below. "Good enough for me. I remember hearing about these boys and those poor girls. Dirty business, that."

Carson nodded.

"Looks like you've got two thousand dollars coming." He grinned. "Minus twenty-five percent. At least, if you're still a deputy."

Carson hesitated. "I don't know if I am or not. If my partner is already back in Fort Smith, I'm probably not."

"Do you want to be?"

Carson looked down at the floor. He had to figure out what to do about Bella. Maybe she would come back with him, and he would do everything in his power to convince her, but somehow in his heart of hearts, he knew she would do what was right for her, and he had to do the same for himself. He looked up and met Deputy Kerr's eyes. "I do."

Deputy Kerr grinned. "I expect Sheriff Greer will be glad to tear up that resignation letter when he hears there's five hundred dollars in it for him."

Carson thought of Bella. "I wonder if he'll want me back right away. I need to see this wagon train through to California."

Deputy Kerr laughed. "How old are you, Deputy?"

"Eighteen and half," Carson said.

"Let me guess. There's a woman involved."

Carson wanted to deny it, but the blood rushing to his face told the truth.

∼

Carson followed Deputy Kerr into one of the stone buildings.

Deputy Kerr walked up to the sergeant sitting behind a polished oak desk in front of a heavy oak door. "He in?"

The sergeant nodded.

"Busy?"

The sergeant stood and poked his head in the door, then stood to one side and motioned them through.

The major, a short, spare man with a fringe of almost-white hair and pale blue eyes, walked around his desk and held out his hand toward Carson. "Major William Bilgely."

"Carson Kettle."

Deputy Kerr said, "United States Deputy Marshal Carson Kettle."

Carson nodded.

After Carson had explained why he'd come to Fort Concho, Major Bilgely said, "I remember that story. Terrible. I'll have some men take them across the river and bury them with the Mexican's you packed in, John."

That evening, after Carson sold the Whatley brother's horses to the owner of the trading post for half of what they'd have been worth back in Fort Smith, Deputy Kerr said, "I reckon that means you're buying supper."

Carson smiled and nodded. "I suppose it does."

A beautiful señorita smiled at Deputy Kerr as they walked into the saloon. Her dark eyes flashed to Carson, then back to Deputy Kerr. She stretched up and pulled a bottle from a high shelf and brought it and two glasses to their table. "Who's your friend, John?" she asked.

Deputy Kerr grinned. "Name's Carson, but y'all don't need to remember it. He's just passing through."

She filled the glasses with amber whiskey. "And what about you, John Kerr? How long are you staying?"

Deputy Kerr placed a familiar hand on her hip and pulled her close. "You know how it is, Maria. I'd stay longer, but this job doesn't give me more'n a moment's rest."

She pulled away.

Deputy Kerr feigned a frown. "Don't be like that. You know I always come back."

She stuck out her lower lip. "But you never stay." She turned away. "I'll fetch you some supper."

Deputy Kerr raised his glass. "To four more evil men in the ground, and to a lost lamb brought back into the fold."

They clinked glasses. Carson smelled the whiskey and sipped in just enough for a taste. The whiskey was smoother than he expected, but nowhere near the quality of some he'd drunk in the past.

Deputy Kerr set his glass on the table and refilled it. He motioned with the neck of his bottle toward Carson's mostly full glass. "Don't like it?"

"It's fine," Carson said. "I'm just more of a sipper."

Maria placed plates in front of them, along with a steaming pot of fragrant stew and a cloth-covered plate of corn tortillas.

Deputy Kerr scooped a spoonful of the stew onto a folded tortilla and took a big bite.

Carson did the same. His mouth burned, and tears formed in his eyes.

Deputy Kerr laughed. "Too much for you?"

Carson coughed. "I'm not used to the peppers."

Deputy Kerr turned toward the bar, where Maria chatted with an old Mexican man. "Maria, darling, bring this boy some buttermilk."

The cool buttermilk soothed Carson's burning lips and tongue.

"Better?" Deputy Kerr asked.

"Much," Carson said with a smile.

As the night wore on, a few men came and went until Carson and Deputy Kerr were the only customers left. Carson yawned over and over. Between his hard ride over the last two days, the whiskey, and the food, he was ready to take the major up on the bed he'd offered.

Glassy-eyed, Deputy Kerr looked past Maria, who now sat on his lap. "We keeping you up?"

Carson smiled and nodded. "It's been a long couple of days. I think my horse is ready for a rubdown and a scoop or two of corn, and I'm ready for my sougan."

"There's a stable out back," Deputy Kerr said. "And rooms upstairs, with feather beds." He looked up at Maria. "I was thinking I might stay here."

Maria shook her head. "Only if you have money for a room."

"I thought I might…"

She shook her head. "I told you last time."

He picked up the clay bottle of tequila from the table and tipped it toward her glass.

She took the bottle from him and plunked it onto the table, then pulled his other hand from her waist and stood up. "Time to close shop."

Deputy Kerr's eyes opened wide and he pushed Maria away with his left hand.

Before Carson could turn his head and follow Kerr's eyes to the door, a heavily accented, Mexican voice said, "Just give us a minute to kill the deputy and his friend, Maria, then we can share some of your tequila, in honor of my dead brothers."

Carson glanced into the mirror behind the bar. Two tall, slim vaqueros stood shoulder to shoulder just inside the doorway, pistols drawn and cocked.

Deputy Kerr's eyes focused as he nodded toward the men. "Evening, gents. I'm surprised to see you here. I thought you'd be back in Mexico by now."

"Who's your friend, Deputy John Kerr?" the vaquero asked.

Kerr bumped Carson's leg with his boot and eased his head to his left, Carson's right. "Just a drifter passing through. He's got nothing to do with any of this. Best let him go."

"It's a bad day for him. He picked the wrong gringo to drink with."

"You wouldn't back-shoot a stranger, would you Enrique?"

Carson watched the men in the mirror while he mentally practiced diving to the floor, flipping the thong from the hammer of his pistol, rolling, and firing. He couldn't die here in this tiny cantina. He had a whole life ahead, and he'd promised Bella he would meet her here.

Enrique grinned. "You know me better than that, Deputy. Of course, I would."

Maria said, "Please don't do this, Enrique. Just come upstairs."

Enrique's eyes flashed toward the young woman. "Why now, Maria? Why the change of heart?"

Carson kicked Deputy Kerr's leg and dove to the floor, drawing his pistol, rolling, and firing, just as he'd rehearsed in his mind. The room exploded with gunfire. Carson's first shot tore into Enrique's ribs and pierced his heart and lungs. He swung his pistol toward the second man, but Deputy Kerr had already shot him twice in the chest.

As the smoke cleared, Maria ran and threw herself into John Kerr's arms and kissed him full on the mouth.

Carson kept his eyes on the door and the windows of the saloon while he reloaded his pistol. He waited, and he waited. When no one else appeared, he glanced at Deputy Kerr and Maria, still locked together. He stepped over the bodies in the doorway, mounted his sorrel, and rode across the river to the fort and his bed.

Despite his weary body, sleep eluded him. At first the trembling excitement of the shooting kept him awake, but soon it was his racing thoughts. What was he doing out here, halfway across Texas? And why was he leaving everyone he loved back in Arkansas? For the first time, he admitted to himself that not everyone he loved was back there. There was one beautiful, dark-eyed beauty he loved, sleeping under a wagon not more than a day or two north. Now that he'd admitted it to himself, he needed to know if she felt the same way. Maybe he'd been hasty in deciding to rejoin the marshals.

14

Bella held the lines over and between her fingers. The hot midday sun beat down on her bonnet like it wanted to cook her brain. Mr. Van Zant sat beside her on the wagon seat, a bottle of the fiery whiskey in his hand. He glanced around the tarp covering her wagon at the train behind them. He seemed better, much better. His breath rose and fell without the recent rattle. Maybe he wasn't dying after all.

Her heart skipped a beat. If he was fit enough to take back leading the wagon train, what would that mean for Carson? Would he continue on with them or ride back to Fort Smith and his mother and father and his brothers and sister? She glanced west. It had been her father's dream to move out to a new land on the Pacific Ocean, and she wanted to be close to him, so she agreed to join him on his adventure. What did she want now? With all that had happened, the only thing she knew for sure was that she wanted to keep Phillip's girls, her girls now, safe. What else mattered? She took the lines in one hand and hugged herself with the other, remembering Carson's arms around her as he comforted her. What had that meant? What did he want? Why had he left the Marshals and stayed on with the wagon train?

"Gate's coming back," Mr. Van Zant said.

Far to the south, Gate loped his bay horse toward them. As he got close, he circled and rode alongside Mr. Van Zant. "There's a dozen shaggies in a little bowl up ahead. If I was to shoot a couple, we'd have enough meat for the whole train for a few days, but we'd be stopped for the rest of the day butchering and putting up the meat.

Mr. Van Zant grinned. "I sure could use a good feed of buffalo tongue." He turned to Bella and grinned. "How are you at gutting and skinning?"

Bella looked at the old man like he was addled. She'd never dressed or gutted anything larger than a chicken.

"Comanche women take care of all that heavy work, while the men slap each other on the back for their good kills and feast on raw liver soaked in bile."

Bella's stomach twisted. She liked liver dredged in flour and fried with onions, but raw and sprinkled with bile?

"I'm just funnin' you.," Mr. Van Zant said. He turned to Gate. "Anywhere to camp?"

Gate nodded. "There's a small creek a mile past the shaggies."

A half-hour later, three shots rang out from somewhere to the west.

Mr. Van Zant turned to Bella. "Hear them bullets smack flesh?" He grinned. "Sounds like we'll be feasting on buffalo 'fore the night's done." He leaned forward. "Pull up a minute. I'll get a couple of the men to ride over and help old Gate with the skinning and gutting."

After three of the men rode west toward the sound of the shooting, Bella pushed her team ahead at a fast walk.

Twenty minutes later, she started her team across the grass and wildflowers on a grassy bench. As they had done so many times before, the other wagons followed and formed a large circle.

Mr. Van Zant said, "You and Gemma unhitch and water the team, but leave them harnessed. We'll take them over and drag back the meat on the hide." He took a sip of whiskey and started around the circle.

After watering the horses, Bella ground drove her team back along the road, following Mr. Corcoran and Abe Waldner, driving their own teams.

Aggy Waldner strolled along beside Bella. "Have you eaten buffalo before?" she asked.

"I tried some salted tongue once. It was alright," Bella replied.

"Abe says the hump meat's the best," Aggy said. "I guess any fresh meat will be good. Since Mr. Van Zant got sick, there ain't been much in the way of fresh meat."

Bella smiled and nodded. "He had a knack for keeping us supplied with venison."

Aggy touched Bella's sleeve and leaned close. "Is he going to make it?"

Bella shrugged. "Seems better today."

"Eva Harker says he's not long for the world and she says if he goes, she's going to insist they drop you from the wagon train."

Bella glanced over. "Why? What have I done to her?"

"She blames you and yours for Vern, and she doesn't like...." Aggy looked at the ground. "She thinks you're an idol worshipper."

Bella touched the front of her dress and the crucifix she always wore.

"There they are," Mr. Corcoran shouted. He clucked his

tongue and pushed his team into a trot and jogged after them.

Big piles of greenish-gray guts lay near each of the buffalo. Gate's bay had a rope tied from the saddle horn to a hind leg of one of the enormous beasts. The taut rope held the buffalo up on its back. Gate and the other men had the animal half skinned. Once they reached the middle of the back with their knives, Gate peeled large chunks of meat from the hind leg and set them on the animal's huge stomach. He continued on and cut away a thick slab of meat from along the backbone, then he cut away the meat from the bones on the animal's hump.

Once he had taken most of the meat from one side of the animal, Gate eased his horse forward, rolled the carcass, and peeled the meat from the other side. Once most of the meat rested, either on the buffalo's paunch or on the clean grass, he dragged the meaty bones away. He turned toward Bella. "Stack the meat on the hide and drag it back to camp."

By the time she stopped the team beside her wagon, flies buzzed and swarmed over every inch of the meat.

"I'll get some pepper," Mr. Van Zant said. He rolled onto his knees and pulled himself to his feet, using the wagon wheel he'd leaned against to steady himself.

Bella untied the hide from the doubletree and tied the team to a wagon wheel. She waved her hands over the meat. For a moment, the flies rose with an angry buzz, then they settled back onto the dark meat.

Mr. Van Zant sprinkled the rest of their pepper over the meat, and most of the flies rose and drifted away on the breeze.

Bella pulled a flour sack rag from the wagon and wrapped it around a foot-long chunk of meat and placed it on one of her tin plates. "I'll be right back." She walked across the opening to the Harker's wagon.

Mrs. Harker sat on the tongue of their wagon and stared at Bella as she approached.

Bella extended the cloth-wrapped meat.

Mrs. Harker sat without reaching for the bundle.

"It's off the backstrap," Bella said. "It should be good."

Without a word, Mrs. Harker turned and faced the other direction.

Bella stood for a moment, unsure what to do. She understood, at least as much as one could understand another's grief, but neither she nor Phillip's girls had done anything to hurt this woman. At least, nothing intentional. She set the plate of meat on the clean grass in the shade of the wagon. "You'll want to salt what you can't use over the next couple of days." When Mrs. Harker said nothing, Bella turned back toward her own wagon. "I guess you knew that."

Gate and Mr. Van Zant divvied the meat amongst the wagons and spent the rest of the afternoon helping Bella and Gemma salt their portion. That evening, the smell of roasting meat filled the air. Bella had taken one tongue for Mr. Van Zant and boiled it until she could peel away the rough gray skin. Once it cooled, she sliced it into thin rounds and fried them in tallow with the last of their potatoes. She fried chunks of tenderloin for Gate and the children and herself.

While the others feasted, she picked at the meat on her plate and stared across at the Harker's wagon. Several of the other women had shared what they had cooked with Mr. Harker and the children. Mrs. Harker stared out into the night from the same spot Bella had left her.

Mr. Van Zant touched Bella's shoulder. "That was fine. Best tongue I ever ate." He cleared his throat. "She's wrong to blame Gabriella or you for what happened. I doubt there's anything you or anyone else can do to bring her back. She'll either find her own way, or she won't."

Bella nodded, but the fear did not leave her. She raised her plate. "Do you want this? I'm not hungry."

Mr. Van Zant said, "You need to eat."

He was right. She took a forkful of meat and potatoes and raised it to her lips, then stopped without tasting it. Something drew her eyes upward.

Across the center of the circle, Mrs. Harker had turned to face her, and even in the flickering firelight, the hatred in her eyes burned across the grassy opening between the wagons.

"I'll have a word with Harker." Mr. Van Zant said. "She doesn't come out of this in the next couple of days, I'm gonna return their money, and they can find their own way to Californy. I never should' a let them rejoin us after the last time." He took a sip of his whiskey. "Must be getting soft in my old age."

"She's grieving," Bella said. "Give her some time."

Mr. Van Zant stood. "There's Harker at Corcoran's wagon. I'll be back."

The next morning, there was not a cloud in the sky. They harnessed early and got on the trail an hour after first light. They had lost half a day getting the meat, and Mr. Van Zant was keen to get in as many miles as possible before the sun reached its peak.

By midmorning, Mr. Van Zant's breath again began to rattle. "I guess I overdid things yesterday. I think I'll crawl in the back and get out of this sun."

At noon, Gate stopped the train to rest the horses and take their midday meal. "Y'all will have to water from your barrels," he shouted. "We'll leave in an hour."

Bella pulled up her team and looked in on Mr. Van Zant. His face shone damp and pale in the light filtering in through the canvas. "Liliana, get Mr. Van Zant some water. Gemma, water the team. Emilia and Gabriella, lay out the meat and biscuits."

Once the girls had laid out the food on a cloth on the tailgate, Bella filled a plate and took it around to the front of the wagon and passed it through to Mr. Van Zant.

He looked up and smiled, but shook his head. "I'm not hungry, but if you could have Liliana fetch me a little more water, I'd be obliged."

Bella sat down beside Gate and the girls in the shade of the wagon and ate the food she had dished for the old wagon boss.

"Look who's coming," Gate said.

Mr. and Mrs. Harker walked up the line of wagons toward them. Mr. Harker handed Bella her plate. He looked at his wife. "Eva has something to say."

At first, Mrs. Harker looked like she might cry, then she glanced around, took a deep breath, and said, "Thank you for bringing us that nice cut of meat." She bit her lips and cast her eyes toward her feet.

"Eva," Mr. Harker said.

Mrs. Harker's face flushed even redder. "We don't blame you or the girl for what happened. It was an accident." Before Bella could say a word, she turned and ran back to her own wagon.

Mr. Harker twisted his hat in his hands. "She's suffering. We all are. Vern was a good boy. I hope you can forgive her."

Bella nodded. "Of course, I can."

Mr. Harker turned and shuffled away, his shoulders stooped as if he'd aged twenty years since they had left Vern buried along the trail.

They watched Mr. Harker until he reached his own wagon. Gate stood and poked his head into the back of the wagon. "I guess laying down the law did some good. I hope it sticks." He set his plate on the tailgate and shouted, "Ten minutes."

15

With nothing else to do, Carson wandered around the light-colored, sandstone buildings comprising Fort Concho. Sturdy and low to the ground, the buildings exuded a sense of permanence and a long-term commitment to this post. A company of buffalo soldiers marched on the large parade ground in the middle of the buildings. Seeing the men's dark, damp faces, and the sweat soaked shirts stuck to their backs, made him glad he'd chosen the marshals over the army.

From time to time, he glanced north, hoping to see the dust stirred by the wagon train, but all he saw was shimmering hot air. He stepped into the shade, leaned against one of the stone buildings, pulled off his hat, and mopped the sweat from his brow with the cuff of his shirt.

He glanced at the cantina and trading post across the river. At some point, Deputy Kerr had moved his horse from the hitching rail. He hadn't seen the deputy since leaving the cantina the night before, and he wanted to discuss how he might get paid for bringing in the Whatleys. Two thousand dollars was a lot of money. Even with a quarter going to Marshal Greer and half of the rest to Gate, he would have $750, plus the $150 he'd got for the Whatleys' horses and saddles.

He fingered the gold coins in his pocket. Before Bella got there, he needed to decide what to do. How could he expect her to come back with him, if he wasn't ready to commit himself to her? And what would he do if she said no... or yes? Was he ready for that type of commitment? What about Phillip's girls? He knew nothing about raising girls.

He wandered north to where he had forded the river on his way in the day before. The dry ground gave way to lush green as the trail sloped down into the river. He leaned against a huge old cottonwood and breathed in the cooler air along the river. He waited and watched. They should be coming any time.

After close to an hour, he turned and walked back toward the fort, stopping at the little adobe, and knocked on the door.

Private George Wright opened the door a crack. "Yes."

Carson hesitated, not sure why he'd even knocked. "Sorry to bother you, but when wagon trains come through here..."

Private Wright opened the door halfway. "Come on in here where it's cool. Once we let the heat in, there's no getting rid of it until nightfall."

Carson stepped inside. The only light came from windows set deep in the walls. A second private sat at a small table. He nodded, pulled a deck of cards from his shirt pocket, and pointed at a chair to his right.

"So, what can we do for you, Deputy?" Private Wright asked.

"Really, nothing," Carson said. "I'm waiting for a wagon

train, and I was just wondering if they cross here or if they go over to the trading post?"

"Usually, they go to the trading post."

Carson turned toward the door. "Alright, then. Thank you."

"Have a seat," Private Wright said. "It's hot outside. You pacing around in that sun won't bring them any quicker. Do you play Old Maid?"

Carson nodded. "I do, but I don't want to be a bother."

"Sit down. We get tired of listening to each other all day."

"I don't want to keep you from your duty," Carson said.

Private Wright grinned. "We been here long enough, the first hoof touches the water, or someone's boots slap the clay coming from the fort, and we slip away the cards and stand to.

Carson sat and played cards until his stomach began to rumble.

Private Wright stood. "Must be dinner time. Come on. Fisher'll keep an eye on things until we come back."

As they walked toward the dining hall, hooves splashing in the river toward the trading post drew Carson's eyes.

Deputy Kerr rode his horse across the river toward them. He grinned when he saw Carson and tipped his hat. "Wright. Deputy."

"We're heading over to eat," Private Wright said. "Will you join us?"

"I've had my dinner, but I'll come have a cup of that fine coffee, old Cooky makes."

Private Wright snorted. "Fine?"

Deputy Kerr laughed. "Put enough sugar in it to float your spoon and it's good as any I ever tasted."

After they'd eaten, Deputy Kerr stood. "I'm heading out. I can write you a letter showing I verified you brought in the Whatleys, but you may have to take it to Denver. That's where the girls were from and that's where you're likely to find their father. Or you could write and include my letter and the others. I'm sure his bank can get the money to yours, but $2000.00 is a lot of money. Might be worth riding to Denver."

Carson looked up from his coffee. Denver. He couldn't go to Denver. He was either going home or he was going to California. How could he go to Denver?

He paced and watched, and paced and checked on the sorrel, until two privates marched out to the little adobe guard shack and Privates Wright and Fisher made their way toward him. He joined them for dinner, but he stirred his plate of ham and beans and scraped most of it into the slop bucket when they left the dining hall. He had ridden hard and fast when bringing the bodies to the fort, but surely, the wagon train should have arrived.

The methodical clip clop of the big horses pulling the wagons and the rhythmic creaks and squeaks of the heavy wagons filled his memory, with the painful slowness of the wagon train. Maybe nothing had happened. Surely, they would be here tomorrow. He retired to his room and sat on the bed. After half an hour, he went to the wash basin on its little stand, washed the sweat and dust from his neck and face and stepped out into the night.

He tied the sorrel outside the cantina and stepped inside. Someone had scrubbed away most of the blood from the floor, but two circles of darker wood, told of what had happened only one night before.

Maria looked up from where she talked to the same old man, she'd been talking to the night before. Her smile brightened her mouth but failed to reach her eyes. She reached for the bottle of whiskey on the high shelf.

Carson shook his head, "Just some of that fire stew, if you got some left and a glass of buttermilk."

This time her smile reached her eyes, as she motioned to the table, he had shared with Deputy Kerr the night before. This time, he took a seat on the side of the table that placed his back against the wall and gave him a view of the door and the windows. As he finished his stew and took a last sip of buttermilk to wash away the burn, the old man nodded and left.

Maria followed him to the door and left it open, allowing in a cool gentle breeze. Then she refilled his buttermilk, poured herself a glass, and sat across from him.

"Thank you," he said. "I think the stew was even better tonight."

She smiled. "I'm glad you enjoyed it, Deputy."

He tried to think of something else to say, but nothing came. He finished his buttermilk and was about to pay and leave.

"What is it about good men?" she asked.

Carson shrugged. "What do you mean?"

"Are you married?"

He shook his head.

"You're young. I heard you say you're from Fort Smith. Is there a woman there?"

His heart sank and his smile fled. "No ma'am."

"You look so sad. Did she leave you?"

"I don't even know what we were, but she was killed."

"I'm sorry," she said. "John says he loves me, but he's always got another outlaw to hunt down."

"It's how we earn our living."

"It might be a living, but it's no life. Sleeping on the

ground. Always watching. Sitting with your back to the wall. John could have died last night...."

Carson didn't know what to say to that. He could have died too. He pressed his lips together and nodded. Then he took a deep breath and said, "People die every day, and someone's got to do what we do. What kind of world would we have if no one went after the thieves and murderers?"

She tilted her head and raised one shoulder. "I just wish it wasn't John."

Carson thought about himself. He knew he didn't want to be a farmer. He'd considered working in a store, but as clean and friendly as that was, deep down he'd known it wasn't for him. Bringing Lijah Penne to justice had brought deep satisfaction and a sense that he had helped make the world a better place. He met her eyes. "I don't know John well, but what else would he do?"

"He could work here. There's much to do."

"Do you think he'd be happy?"

She shook her head.,"He's always happy when he comes, but after a few days, I feel his restlessness. He's like a panther. He loves the hunt."

Carson slipped off into his own thoughts. What kind of life could he offer Bella? Even if she came back to Fort Smith, he would always be riding off into the territories. Marshal Greer had a wife, and she appeared happy. But Marshal Greer, long past his manhunting days, spent his time in Fort Smith, and sent out Carson and the other deputies.

"I should close up," Maria said, jerking him from his thoughts.

As he rode toward the river crossing and the fort, galloping hooves from the north broke over the buzz of insects and the rustling breeze. The hoofbeats turned to splashing, as the galloping horse hit the north crossing without slowing.

"Halt!" One of the privates from the adobe guard house shouted.

Carson dug his heels into the sorrel's ribs and pushed him into the river and across toward the fort.

16

Carson arrived at the officers' quarters just as Gate and a private stopped in front of Major Bilgely's door. The private stepped to the door and tapped his knuckles against the door. "Sir?"

Gate pushed the private aside and banged on the door. "It's Gate Rudd, Major. We need your sawbones."

Carson's breath caught in his throat. He leaped from the sorrel and ran to the door, just as the Major, dressed in a long night shirt, opened it. "What's happened, Rudd?"

Carson interrupted and grabbed Gate by the shoulder. "Who is it?"

"It's old Clifford Van Zant," Gate said. "I'm afraid he's dying."

Carson breathed out a sigh, relieved it wasn't Bella or one of the girls.

"How far out are you?" the major asked.

"Twenty miles. Give or take."

The major looked at Gate and shook his head. "Doctor Wilton broke his leg last week. There's no way he can ride that far. I doubt he could even do it in a wagon."

"Clifford's awful bad. I don't believe he'll make the trip here without some help from a doctor."

The major stepped out the door. "Let's go talk to the good doctor. I'll leave it to him."

Carson followed along as the others trotted to the other side of the compound. He prayed to himself. 'Please God. Let Mr. Van Zant live.' He ran through his memories. What had he promised Mr. Van Zant? He hadn't offered or committed to leading the wagon train. Mr. Van Zant had put him in charge of, without asking his permission. But he'd taken the job, and someone had to get the settlers to California. Gate knew the way, but he was right when he said he didn't have the patience to nurse the bickering, sometimes whining group halfway across the country.

A half-hour later, Carson and Gate helped the doctor into the back of a buckboard and onto the bed of blankets they had arranged to give him a modicum of comfort. The doctor grimaced and lifted his still-splinted leg with his hands. "Put a couple of those folded blankets under there."

While Carson arranged the blankets Major Bilgely set the black leather medical bag over the side of the buckboard. "You don't have to do this, Harlan. Sounds like old Clifford's done for anyway."

The doctor placed a hand on the Major's. "I'll be fine, Will."

Gate climbed into the seat and lifted the reins. "Alright then." He shook the reins and started the team into trot.

"Easy!" Doctor Wilton said, as the steel-shod, wooden wheels bounced over a set of dried ruts in front of the stable.

Gate eased the horses back into a gentler jog.

After stopping several times to let the doctor change position and sip on a bottle of laudanum, they were less than halfway back to the wagon train, when the sun breached the eastern horizon. An hour later, the first of the wagons appeared, coming their way.

Carson galloped ahead and met Mr. and Mrs. Harker leading the convoy. He stopped the sorrel. "We've got the doctor. Where is he?"

Mr. Harker stared straight ahead and slapped the reins on the wide rumps of his roans. "Dead. Good as anyway."

Mr. Braxton rode up on his big dun horse, his long-barreled goose gun resting over the pommel of his saddle and pointing uncomfortably in Carson's direction.

Carson glanced down the line of wagons. "Where is he?"

Mr. Corcoran motioned over his shoulder with his chin.

Carson galloped down the line of wagons until he came to the last wagon, the one belonging to the Waldners.

Abe's face shone bright red, even through his deep suntan. He pulled off his hat, showing the distinct line between where the sun hit his face and his hat covered his white forehead. Before Carson could say anything, Abe said, "I tried to stop them, but she wouldn't have it. She told us to go on. Said she wanted nothing more to do with them."

Carson struggled to understand what Abe was saying.

Aggy Waldner looked up at Carson. "We offered to stay after they drove on, but she went mad. Pulled a little pocket gun on us. Said she'd kill us both if we didn't leave."

"Where is she," Carson shouted. "Is she alright?"

The Waldners both pointed back along the road. "She was out of her head but sound of body."

Tears welling in her eyes, Aggy turned to her husband. "We should have stayed with her. She wouldn't have shot us."

Carson didn't wait to hear Abe's reply. Instead, he whipped the sorrel with the tails of his reins and ran the horse as hard as he could go, north along the trail.

The grays, still hitched to Bella's wagon, stood hipshot and swatting flies with their little, short tails. Bella, up to her knees in a fresh grave, raised her eyes as he rode closer. Clothing and bedding and books and a broken sack of flour and other food lay scattered around the wagon. The four girls stopped gathering things and watched him ride up.

Gabriella ran toward him, her eyes red and puffy. "He's dead, Carson, and they threw our things all over and they left us. Said they hoped the Comanches got us all." She burst into tears.

Carson stepped from the still stopping sorrel, scooped her up as he ran by, and cradled her head against his shoulder. He skidded to a stop beside the grave Bella dug. "What happened?"

Bella looked at him with dry, rage-filled eyes, but the clean streaks cutting a trail through the dirt on her cheeks told of recent tears. "Just like she said." She pounded the shovel into the hard clay and scraped up a meager load of dirt.

Carson set Gabriella down, stepped into the hole, and took the shovel from Bella's blistered and bleeding hands. "I'll do this, but let's get him out of the wagon and you can get him cleaned up, while I dig. Gate and the doctor will be along soon."

Mr. Van Zant lay under a blanket on his side in the back of the wagon. Bella's things that hadn't been tossed out, lay strewn and scattered around the body.

"What happened,? Carson asked.

"They were looking for his money."

"Did they find it?"

She nodded, "I saw Corcoran hold up a leather satchel that wasn't mine. He and Harker spoke, and they all left.

"Tears filled her eyes and spilled down the trails on her cheeks.,"I should have stopped them."

"You couldn't stop a mob like that."

"I had your pistol, but Braxton just sat his horse with a stupid grin on his face, pointing that bird gun of his from me to each of the girls."

Carson stared south down the road. His vision narrowed and he glanced at the Yellowboy in its scabbard on the grazing sorrel. He burned to remount and ride after them and make them pay for what they'd done. Instead, he wrapped his arms around Bella and said, "You did right."

Her entire body jerked as she sobbed against his neck, then she took a deep breath, pushed herself back, wiped the tears from her cheeks, and said, "Help me get him down."

By the time they had Mr. Van Zant laid out, in the shade of the wagon, on his own blanket. Gate drove the army team and buckboard over the rise. As he stopped the team near Bella's wagon, The Waldners and the McChesneys stopped their horses fifty yards behind him.

Carson left Bella beside Mr. Van Zant's body and trotted over to greet Gate and the doctor. "We're too late."

Gate nodded back toward the wagons behind him. "So they told me." He frowned. "If the doc hadn't been with me, I'd 'a taken the shotgun from that fool Braxton and made him swaller it."

Carson nodded then looked at the Waldners and McChesneys sitting solemn and eyes down on their wagon seats.

Gate looked over his shoulder. "They don't want anything to do with what happened here. Said they would have stayed but Bella insisted they go." He held up his fingers in the form of a pistol.

Bella turned her head until her bonnet hid her face. "I hope they know I wouldn't have done it."

Gate laughed but there was little humor in it. "They asked me to make sure you were okay with them coming back."

She nodded without looking up from Mr. Van Zant.

Gate turned and waved the two wagons forward.

In little time, with Carson, Gate, Abe Waldner, and Luke McChesney digging, the grave was ready.

Carson jumped into the hole and took Mr. Van Zant under the arms and eased his stiffening body to the flat bottom. He reached up, and Gate and Abe took his hands and pulled him from the grave.

Bella found her family Bible and extended it to the men. Each in turn, shook his head, until Carson took the heavy old book. He turned to the 23rd Psalm and read:

"The Lord is my shepherd; I shall not want. He maketh me to lie down in green pastures: he leadeth me beside the still waters. He restoreth my soul: he leadeth me in the paths of righteousness for his name's sake. Yea, though I walk through the valley of the shadow of death, I will fear no evil: for thou art with me; thy rod and thy staff they comfort me. Thou preparest a table before me in the presence of mine enemies: thou anointest my head with oil; my cup runneth over. Surely goodness and mercy shall follow me all the days of my life: and I will dwell in the house of the Lord for ever."

He looked up from the book and then glanced into the grave. "Old Mr. Van Zant was a good man. Those folks didn't kill him. God took him, but they did him wrong in his dying, and they did wrong to this woman and these children." He thumbed ahead a few pages to the 28th Psalm and read:

"Give them according to their deeds, And according to the wickedness of their endeavours: Give them after the work of their hands; Render to them their desert."

"Amen," Gate and Bella said in unison.

The Waldners and the McChesneys looked from Caron to Bella to each other. They all nodded and said, "Amen."

Bella took a shovel from the pile of dirt and began throwing shovelful after shovelful into the grave.

Carson touched her elbow and stopped her. Without a word, he reached out and took the shovel. The other men each pitched in and soon the grave was mounded and tamped.

Carson looked around. "I guess we'll pack up the rest of Bella's things and head south."

They stopped for the night at a little creek a few miles on. Grim-faced, Bella stepped from her wagon, dropped the lines over her shoulder and unhooked the trace chains holding her team to the wagon.

Carson wrapped his reins around the wagon wheel and took the heavy driving lines from her. "Let Doctor Wilton have a look at your hands."

While the doctor ministered to Bella's torn hands, Mrs. Waldner and Mrs. McChesney started supper.

Carson walked past Bella's wagon and downstream a hundred yards and slipped in behind a clump of brush. Thinking of Mr. Van Zant, he slid the thong from the hammer of his Smith and Wesson and drew, cocked, and aimed twenty times. Then, he checked the loads and walked back to camp.

"Supper's ready," Aggy Waldner said.

"Thank you," Carson said. "You folk go ahead. I've got something I need to tend to." He pulled a bridle from the back of Bella's wagon and walked out and caught Mr. Van Zant's horse.

Gate met him halfway back to the wagons. "I know what you're thinking, but let it go. I know Clifford lost his wife and daughter and he's got no close kin for that money."

Carson pushed by. "I can't just let them get away with what they did to Bella and the girls."

Gate nodded and reached for the reins. "Catch your sorrel. I know he's tired, but they won't have gone too far, and we've got all night."

"I want you to stay and look after them," Carson said, looking at Bella and the girls.

Bella looked back at him with questions and concern in her eyes.

Gate took the reins from Carson. "Waldner and McChesney are good men. They'll be fine until we get back."

17

Carson and Gate galloped along the road, their Winchesters in hand, and resting over the front of their saddles. As the last hints of daylight passed, they slowed to a trot. Stopping each time they found themselves on high ground, they scanned ahead for the wagon train. After riding for two more hours, they spotted the flickering light of a fire reflecting off grayish-white wagon covers standing against a dark line of trees marking a creek.

"I thought they'd go further," Gate said.

Carson nodded and pulled his horse into a walk.

"Got a plan?" Gate asked.

"We'll take our time. Wait until they're sleeping, then go in and get the money back."

"They'll be ready for us."

"I suppose," Carson said. "I don't want to kill anybody, though there's some…. Let's sneak in on foot. Harker's bound to have the money, unless they've already divvied it up."

Gate spat on the ground. "Bunch of fools. Not one of them been over the trail, and they still got a lot of desert and some mountains to cross. Us killing them would be a quicker end to their suffering."

They rode on until they could see the outline of the people in the flickering light reflecting off the wagon covers. Carson steered his sorrel in behind a clump of brush. "Let's wait here until they're good and asleep."

"The fools is all gathered around one fire, like they're having a party. Surely, they knew we'd be coming after 'em," Gate said.

"I don't hear them laughing," Carson said. "Maybe something happened."

Gate grunted. "Maybe just waiting for us."

Hours later, Carson lay on his back, staring at the bright, three-quarter moon. He glanced south. The fire had burned down and, as far as he could see, no one stirred. Maybe Gate was right. Maybe they should forget the money and let the desert and the mountains take care of these fools. He sat up. No. They would take care of it here and now.

Gate glanced at him. "Time?"

Carson nodded. "I should take them in and let a judge decide, but who knows how long that might take and what the judge might decide to do with Mr. Van Zant's money. I say we take half the money. Best I can tell, we're close to halfway to California. We'll give the Waldners and the McChesneys back all their money and give the rest to Bella for her and the girls. I think old Van Zant would like that."

Gate nodded. "I wouldn't give them back a dime, but whatever you think." He crawled to his feet and checked the load in his Winchester.

Carson slid the thong from his pistol.

They stooped low and trotted along a shallow draw that ran parallel to the road and ended near the little tree-lined creek running below the circled wagons.

They crept along the edge, pausing often to look and listen. Horses stirred and snorted, night birds sang, and insects buzzed. As they got closer, snores and then even heavy breathing reached them.

Gate thrust his arm in front of Carson and stopped him. He pointed. Mr. Harker sat on the tongue of his wagon, staring away from them, out into the darkness.

Carson eased his Smith and Wesson from his holster and crept forward until he was right behind the man. He whispered, "Not a word," at the same time, he pressed the barrel of his pistol against Mr. Harker's back.

Mr. Harker chuckled. "Wondered when you'd get here, but y'all are too late."

Carson glanced at Gate, then pressed his pistol harder into Harker's back. "What do you mean?"

"It's all gone."

"The money?"

"What else? Braxton shot Corcoran. Killed him dead. Took all Van Zant's money, then made us all dig out our own pokes and give that to him too. He's been watching when we traded along the way. He knew where most of us hid our money. When he rode off, he said he'd kill anyone who followed him."

Carson stepped around Mr. Harker until he could see his eyes. "He took all of it?"

Mr. Harker nodded and dropped his face into his hands.

"I thought he was your friend," Carson said.

"We thought so too," Mr. Harker said. "He was never warm, but he kept bringing in those birds and rabbits for the pot."

The Harker's wagon shifted, and Carson swung his pistol.

Mrs. Harker climbed out of the wagon.

Even in the dim glow of the moon, it was clear she'd been struck. Her right eye was swollen shut, and a gash along her cheek oozed dampness.

"What happened?"

"I tried to stop him," she said. "The rest of these cowards wasn't doing nothing."

Mr. Harker rubbed his shoulder as he stared at the ground. "I still got Corcoran's blood on me. Sprayed out of him, like a stuck pig. He was dead before he hit the ground."

Carson glanced at Mrs. Harker and thought of Bella. A flicker of joy coursed through his body. If anyone deserved this, it was Mrs. Harker. He bowed his head. With all she'd been through, part of him wanted to be sorry for his thoughts, but he wasn't.

He holstered his pistol. "Which way did he go?"

They both pointed west.

Gate stood up from where he had squatted. "Let's go get our horses." He glanced east. "Be an hour or so before it's light enough for tracking."

They trotted back along the road toward their horses.

Carson turned to Gate. "We need to tell Bella and the others what's happening."

Gate shook his head. "No time or horsepower for that. They'll figure out what we're doing."

Carson stopped and sprinted back toward the wagon train.

The Harkers still sat on the tongue of their wagon, and a few of the others had joined them.

Carson skidded to a stop. "One of you needs to go back and tell the other's what's happened. Tell them we've gone after Braxton. Tell them to wait for us at Fort Concho."

Mr. Harker looked up without saying a word.

"I'm holding you responsible, Harker. Someone doesn't get word to them, you're the one that's going to pay."

After hesitating a moment, Mr. Harker glanced at his wife, then said, "We'll let them know."

"Start someone back there, now. Make sure they know to watch out for Braxton."

∽

As THE LINE of sunlight hit the dry ground to the west of the wagon train, Carson and Gate rode in a slow circle until Gate pointed at a line of tracks heading west. "What do you see?" He asked, looking at Carson.

"One horse."

"And?"

Carson leaned over. "One of the hooves toes out?"

"Which one?"

"One of the lefts."

"Front or back?"

Carson thought back to learning to shape the shoes he had nailed onto horses. The toed-out hoof was more pointed than the other. "It's the left rear."

Gate nodded, glanced along the line of tracks west, then followed them. "There's nothing that way. So, what does that mean?"

"He'll likely circle."

"Which way?"

"Might keep heading south and west, but.... There's no way to tell, is there?"

"Nope," Gate said. "So, what does that mean?"

"We can't try to cut him off. We'll have to stay on his tracks."

Gate nodded.

Braxton's tracks led them to the banks of the Concho River, then into the water.

Gate stopped his horse and looked up and down the river. "What do you see?"

"Nothing," Carson said.

"And what does that tell you?"

Carson knew the trick of riding in a river to hide tracks. In fact, he had used it himself. "He's hiding his tracks."

"Which way did he go?"

Carson examined the river, trying to see if there was anything that might give him a hint. Finally, he shook his head.

"If I were betting," Gate said, "I'd bet downstream."

"Why?" Carson asked.

"Muddy-bottomed river like this, a horse stirs up a cloud of silt that flows downstream with the water. Man with a sharp eye might see that."

"How long would that last?" Carson asked.

Gate shook his head. "Hard to say. Depends how long he's in the river and what's on the bottom. There's another thing."

Carson looked and waited.

"He's going to need supplies."

Again, Carson was thinking without speaking.

Gate sat his horse, watching and waiting.

Carson glanced over. "He didn't take a packhorse, and it's a long haul back to Miss Berta's. Closest place to get anything is the trading post at Fort Concho."

Gate nodded. "We'll start downstream. Most don't stay in the water too long. You take this side and I'll take the other. Stay up out of the brush and watch for tracks or broken branches or anything else. Call me over if there's any doubt."

Carson nodded and started Mr. Van Zant's big brown.

"Don't git ambushed, either," Gate said. "I don't wanna have to tell Miss Bella I got you killed."

Carson glanced over at the older man. What did he mean by that?

They rode along the river for half an hour.

Gate whistled.

Carson jerked his Yellowboy from the scabbard as he looked all around. He rode a few yards higher up the bank until he could see the far side.

Gate pointed downstream and waved him forward, then started his own horse in the direction he'd pointed.

Braxton's horse stood, only his neck and head above the water, in the middle of the river.

Carson scanned the area. There was no sign of Braxton.

Gate waved him down toward the river.

Carson was about to enter the water and check on Braxton's horse when Gate shouted, "Quicksand!"

Carson pulled up short of the water. "What do we do?"

Gate pulled out his Winchester, jacked in a round, and aimed at the trapped horse.

"Wait," Carson said. "He'll hear us."

"Knows we're coming, already," Gate said.

Carson hated the thought of killing the horse. "Let me see if I can get him out of there."

Gate shook his head, but lowered his rifle.

Carson slipped out of his boots and clothes and slid into the murky water. Slick, silty mud oozed between his toes and sucked at his feet. He thrust himself forward until he was swimming. When he got to the horse, he uncoiled the rope hanging from his shoulder and tied a bowline around the horse's neck. He swam back to shore, dragging the tail of the rope with him.

He eased Mr. Van Zant's horse forward until the river water reached its knees. He dallied the rope around his saddle horn, and pulling on the reins, asked the big brown to back up.

When the rope came tight, the horse in the river thrashed his head, spraying water in every direction.

Carson pulled harder on the reins and squeezed with his legs.

The big brown leaned against the rope until his haunches sank near to the ground.

Braxton's horse thrashed and tossed his head, but stayed stuck.

Carson was about to give up when the brown groaned and gave one more mighty pull.

Braxton's horse spun toward him and splashed over onto his side in the muddy water. The brown dropped onto his haunches, then rose and scrambled up the bank, dragging Braxton's horse with him.

Braxton's horse stepped out of the water, shook, spraying Carson and the brown with water, then dropped his head into the grass along the river as if nothing had happened.

18

Staying on his own side of the river, Carson burned to lean low over his horse's neck and spur him forward. The only thing slowing him was the threat that Braxton might lie in ambush for them. Still, he and Gate, one on each side of the river, galloped toward Fort Concho, slowing only when the terrain offered a good opportunity for someone to lie in wait. Braxton would need a horse, a saddle and supplies, and Fort Concho was the closest place to get all those things.

Carson pushed his horse across the rocky ford, not toward the fort, but toward the trading post. Gate held up a hand and stopped him.

A body lay in the dust outside the trading post, a pool of blood spreading from it.

Wispy gray hair blew in the breeze. "Looks to be the trader," Carson said.

Gate nodded. "Old Jesse. Been here a long time."

Carson's heart jumped as he thought of Maria. He glanced back at Gate. "Think Braxton's still here?"

Gate shrugged his shoulders. "Be best we circle and see if there's fresh tracks heading south. Better yet, you wait here and watch. Get your Sharps ready and if he pops out of the trading post or the cantina or the stable out back, let him have it."

Carson nodded, dismounted, pulled the Sharps from its saddle boot, and checked that there was a round chambered. He glanced around for a rest for the heavy rifle, then sat and rested his elbows on his knees, just as his father had taught him.

Gate kept his Winchester in hand as he galloped a wide circle around the buildings. Once he reached the road south, he dismounted, squatted, and outlined something in the dust with his finger. He stood and raised a hand, telling Carson to stay where he was. He sprinted to the edge of the cantina, up onto the porch, glanced in the closest window, then sprinted past and threw open the door and darted inside.

He ducked back out and did the same thing with the trading post, then popped back out the door and waved. "Come on. He's gone."

Carson leaped onto the brown, picked up the reins on Braxton's dun, and hustled to the trading post.

Gate knelt beside Old Jesse, the trader. "Cut his throat. Must'a surprised him."

"Probably didn't want to risk the soldiers hearing a shot," Carson said. He glanced at the cantina, then spurred his horse forward.

"She ain't in there," Gate shouted. "Unless she's hiding."

Carson burst through the door, his pistol drawn. He glanced left and right, then ran through the swinging doors to the kitchen. "Maria!"

He backed out and bounded up the stairs, two at a time. He paused at the top. "Maria?"

Still no answer.

"Braxton. If you're in here, you might as well come out."

"There was three sets of tracks heading south. I think he took her."

Carson ran down the hall and burst into each of the three small bedrooms. The last one smelled of Maria and rose water, but she wasn't there. He bounded down the stairs, past Gate standing in the middle of the floor, and out to the horses.

"Hold up," Gate said. "There's horses in the corral out back. He's riding fresh mounts. We'd best switch. Old Jesse won't care no more. Take Braxton's horse and hustle over and tell the major what happened, while I switch our saddles onto fresh horses."

Carson hesitated, then threw himself onto Braxton's dun and drove him across the river toward the fort. He skidded to a stop just as the major stepped from the dining hall. "Old Jesse's been killed," Carson said. "Man named Ned Braxton. We think he's got Maria."

"I'll get some men mounted," the major said.

Carson spun the horse back toward the trading post. "They headed south." He splashed the dun back through the river and around to the stable and corrals just in time to see Gate lead out two of the three Whatley horses he had sold the trader only days before. He quickly stripped the saddle from Braxton's dun, dropped it into the dirt, and turned the horse into the corral with Mr. Van Zant's brown and Gate's bay.

They stayed on the road, Gate following the tracks as easily as a man of letters might follow the words in a children's book. At a line of scattered manure, Gate dragged the mustang he rode to a stop. Keeping the reins in his hand, he bent over and pressed his fingers into the damp manure. "Keep your eyes open. They're not long gone."

They rode ahead, eyes flashing left and right. Gate pointed ahead at a moving plume of dust, then leaned forward and laid his heels to his horse.

Carson's horse easily passed the little gray Gate rode. "I'll see if I can get around him," he shouted as he galloped by and eased off into the dusty ground, his horse dodging clumps of mesquite and cedar.

He angled southwest and lashed his horse with the tails of the reins. After a few hundred yards, it was clear the Whatley horse, though quick to start, did not have enough bottom to hold pace. Carson eased into a trot until the horse's heaving sides slowed a little.

He pushed back into a slow lope and, as they topped a low rise, glanced back at Gate, now only a few hundred yards back. The plume of dust, if anything, was even further away.

The relentless sun beat down, but Carson kept the horse going. He couldn't let Braxton get away with Maria. He thought of the coins he carried in his saddlebags and hoped they would come to a ranch where he could buy a better horse.

He angled back to the road and settled in beside Gate. An hour later, they came to a ranch gate, with a half-mile long two-track trail leading to an adobe cabin and barn nestled in a green oasis of cottonwood trees. The tracks led from the main road toward the buildings.

Gate slowed his horse and motioned to his right. "Get around that hill and see if you can get above him. Use your Sharps if you can."

Carson nodded.

Gate steered off the road to the left and Carson headed right, toward the backside of the hill. He rode past a few red and white, long-horned cattle grazing on scattered bunches of gamagrass, until he reached a clump of mesquite he had marked as being across the hill from the buildings. He tied his weary mount, though it was unlikely the horse would wander far, given the way his head drooped toward the ground.

Carson took his Sharps and trotted up the hill, stopping just before the crest. He glanced over through the multi-leaved fronds of a low mesquite bush.

Two bodies sprawled in front of the adobe cabin.

Gate waved his arms and pointed south at a plume of dust, not far gone.

Seeing half a dozen horses in a corral attached to the barn, Carson sprinted down the hill to his tired mount, shoved the Sharps back in its boot, leaped into the saddle, and pulled his Yellowboy. The horse groaned but leaped forward and galloped up and around the hill.

As the ranch buildings came into sight, Carson skidded the horse to a stop.

Maria stood in the shade of the porch. Behind her, Braxton stood in the doorway, his shotgun pressed into Maria's back. "Step on up here, boys. I'd hate to cut this pretty señorita in half. I got other plans for her."

Hands bound before her and a gag in her mouth, Maria shook her head, warning them with her eyes.

Braxton slid the shotgun up Maria's back to her neck. "Both of you drop them rifles. Right now. I'll count to three."

Gate had his rifle pointed at Braxton, but Carson was sure he wouldn't shoot. Not with the business end of Braxton's bird gun pressed into Maria's neck.

Carson wondered if Braxton looked away, could he possibly risk a shot, and decided he could not. He tossed his Yellowboy onto a clump of low-growing cedar.

"Keep your hands high and ride on in, so's I can see you better," Braxton shouted.

Both Carson and Gate eased their tired horses forward. Carson thought of the Derringer he normally carried but had left with Bella. There was no way Braxton would or could let any of them live.

He stopped the horse.

"Keep coming, Deputy," Braxton said.

"Let the girl go and I'll give you a running start."

Braxton laughed and shook his head.

"I give you my word. That's Deputy U.S. Marshal John Kerr's woman you've got there. You hurt her, he'll leave no rock unturned."

Braxton laughed again. But there was no humor in it. "Nobody knows I've got her, but you two."

Carson glanced north over his shoulder. "Major Bilgely and his men know who we were chasing."

"William King Crown's my real name," Braxton said with a laugh. "I picked Ned Braxton off'n a tombstone. Needs be, I'll pick another."

"Even if you walk out of here, Deputy Kerr won't stop until you're in the ground."

Braxton grinned and glanced from Carson and Gate and back. "Come on in a little closer, and we can talk about it. One!"

Carson knew Braxton needed them to come into range of the shotgun, but it seemed he had no choice. If they didn't do what the outlaw said, they might well kill him, but Maria would die, and he couldn't allow that.

"Two!"

Carson started the tired horse forward.

"Keep coming," Braxton said.

Carson found Maria's eyes and lowered his own eyes toward the ground at her feet.

She narrowed her eyes.

Again, he glanced down at her feet.

She gave a slight nod.

Just as they came into range of the shotgun, Carson nodded his head and threw himself from his horse. Maria sprawled to the ground, bumping Braxton with her backside as she pushed away.

Braxton's shotgun barked and lead pellets ripped a chunk of dry sod from the spot Carson had just scrambled away from.

Gate drew his pistol, fired, and missed.

Braxton turned his shotgun on Gate.

Carson's first bullet slammed into Braxton's shoulder, spoiling his aim. His second shot tore through the outlaw's bicep and into his chest, ending his life.

Once the smoke and the excitement of the battle had settled, they found a small, fenced burial plot in the shade of the spreading branches of an old live oak near the spring and started digging graves for the older couple Braxton had killed.

Major Bilgely and a dark-skinned sergeant galloped into the yard, leading eight buffalo soldiers. The major dismounted near the blanket-wrapped bodies and asked, "Are Edward and Emma both dead?"

Maria looked up from where she sat in the shade and nodded.

The major tipped his hat toward Maria. "Braxton kill them?"

She nodded again.

"I'm sad to hear that. They were good folks." He turned to the sergeant. "Have the men finish these graves. I'll say a few words over these good folks once they're done." He turned toward the adobe cabin. "Let's get out of this heat while they dig. Edward and Emma won't mind."

Once they had laid the old couple to rest, the soldiers set out their bedrolls in the shade near the spring, while Maria cooked up beef and beans they found in the cabin.

The next morning, after bacon and more beans, they rode back to Fort Concho.

Carson and Gate left the soldiers and accompanied Maria back to the cantina. Old Jesse's body had been buried, and the trading post had been closed up and appeared to be secure and in order.

Carson turned to Gate and Maria. "I'm riding out to check on Bella and the girls."

"Want me to come with you?" Gate asked.

Carson shook his head. "Why don't you stay here and help until Maria figures things out."

Gate nodded.

With no customers, they closed the doors to the trading post. Gate and Maria wandered into the cantina for a drink while Carson saddled Mr. Van Zant's brown horse.

He tied up out front and carried in the heavy pouch of gold coin and greenbacks they had found on Braxton. "When Harker and his crew come in, keep fifty dollars a wagon and a hundred for McChesney and Waldner. Let them sort out the rest."

Gate frowned. "You sure about this? Way I see it, after what they did to Bella and those girls, they don't deserve a thing."

Carson nodded. "I won't have them say we took what wasn't ours."

The same old Mexican, who regularly drank pulque and visited with Maria, wandered through the door. "Wagons coming."

Carson bounded outside, then stopped and returned. "It's Harker and the rest."

19

Carson's horse spooked as a gang of little boys broke from between the cantina and the trading post. He laughed, squared himself back in the saddle, trotted on and hit the Concho River just as the Harker's team broke out of the water.

Mr. Harker lowered his eyes and stared at the stripes of darker hair running down the center of the broad, red rumps of his mules.

Mrs. Harker, her left eye still swollen shut and her cheek shining red, purple, and yellow, looked up with defiance in her eyes. "You catch that devil?"

Carson wanted to ride on, but he reined up his horse and nodded.

"You get our money?" she asked with a snarl.

Carson ignored her question and her tone. "Where's Mrs. Foresti and her girls?"

Mr. Harker laid a firm hand on his wife's arm. "They're at the tail end of the train. We decided..." He looked at his wife. "We all decided we were wrong to leave them alone."

Mrs. Harker looked like she'd swallowed a toad, but she held her tongue.

"Move on, 'fore we get stuck," one of the other teamsters shouted from the river.

Carson cupped his hand over his eyes and stared north, but the rise on the far side of the river blocked his view of the last third of the wagon train. He turned to Mr. Harker. "Gate's at the cantina beside the trading post. We'll meet there."

Mr. Harker clucked his tongue, slapped his reins on his mules, and led the train forward.

Carson urged his horse down the steep bank beside the cut for the road and plunged into the water, spraying the driver of the next wagon in line. "Sorry," he shouted as he pushed the horse hard across the water.

Most of the men lowered their eyes to the backs of the teams they drove as he rode past. At least they still had enough of a conscience to show some shame for what they'd done.

There was about fifty yards of open road between the last wagon and the Waldner's wagon. Behind the Waldners, Bella drove her team, followed by Mr. McChesney and his family.

Gemma, Liliana, and Emilia saw him coming, left the Waldner and McChesney children, and ran toward him, shouting his name.

With Gabriella sleeping beside her, her little dark head buried in the full skirt of her lap, Bella looked up from under the brim of her bonnet and smiled a shy smile.

Carson's heart raced, and he found it difficult to breathe. Suddenly, he didn't know what to say. "We caught Braxton. I'm fine. Gate's alright too." He struggled to find the words to show her how happy he was to see her, but instead glanced over his shoulder at the wagons and said, "I'd best get back to the cantina, before they overrun poor old Gate."

Bella nodded and touched the brake lever on her wagon as her team started down the slope into the river.

Carson, worried about Bella driving the team through the now-rutted river bottom, rode beside the grays as they splashed through the river.

Bella handled the team with ease, urging them to pull harder anytime the wagon started to sink into the river bottom, and soon she slapped the reins on their big backsides and urged them up out of the water. As the water streamed from their gray hides, she looked up at Carson. "Get going. We can talk later."

By the time Carson reached the cantina, Mr. Harker had his team unhitched and was leading them to the main fork of the river for water. Instead of tending to a fire or her children, Mrs. Harker started for the cantina, stopped and turned back to her wagon, then turned once again toward the cantina.

Carson tied his horse and hurried inside. He pulled his pistol and checked the loads.

Gate looked up from the stacks of coins he had lined up on the bar with questions in his eyes.

Carson shrugged. "Just in case." He turned to Maria. "Do you have enough water drawn for everyone?"

"I do," she said.

Carson glanced over his shoulder, then back at Maria. "Nothing but water, or maybe coffee, until we've done our business."

Mrs. Harker opened the door and peered in.

"Come in," Carson said.

"I'll wait for the others," she said.

"Suit yourself, but it's a little cooler out of the sun,"

Carson said. He glanced back. "This is Maria." His cheeks warmed when he realized he didn't know Maria's last name.

Mrs. Harker glared toward the back of the room, then backed away and closed the door.

It was almost a half hour before all the men and most of the women stood shoulder to shoulder inside the little cantina.

Maria flitted around, handing out whiskey glasses and beer mugs of water.

"Enough waiting," Mrs. Harker said. "Everybody who matters is here."

Carson glanced around the room. Neither Bella, nor the Waldners, nor the McChesneys were in the cantina. His face burned and his heart stuck in his throat. He picked up the sack that had held Mr. Van Zant's money and stepped toward the bar. He reached out as if to sweep all the money Gate had divvied and stacked into the bag.

Gate grabbed his arm and shook his head.

Mr. Harker pushed past his wife and stepped forward. "We all met last night." He glanced at the door. "Most all of us. We decided to let you keep all the money we paid Mr. Van Zant if y'all will lead us to California."

Carson, still angry, swelled. He was about to tell them to go to Hell, when Gate touched his arm and said, "We'll need some time to think about that." He looked toward the bar. "In the meantime, we've divvied up half the money y'all paid Clifford."

"Half?" Mrs. Harker shouted. "What about the rest?"

By now Carson had caught his breath and stepped forward. "Be glad we're giving you half, after what you did." He stepped forward until he almost touched her. He met her one glaring eye and held his eyes on her until she looked away and stepped back a half step. "We got you more than halfway."

A man in a floppy hat shouted from the back of the crowd, "We paid to get taken all the way. Way I see it, we don't owe nothing until we're dippin' our toes in the Pacific."

Gate stepped forward, his Winchester now in his hands.

This time, Carson stopped his friend. "You have two choices." he laid his hand on his pistol and spoke over the murmuring crowd. "Take your half share now, and travel on without us, or wait until we've had the night to think about going on with you. The rest of the money and things we found on Braxton are in those saddlebags," he said, pointing toward a table against the back wall.

A murmur rose as the travelers edged toward the saddlebags. Mr. Harker raised one hand and shouted. "We already talked this over. We voted. We can follow the road as well as the next, fella, but there's a desert and mountains bigger than any of us have seen to cross. We need these men. I say we wait until tomorrow and pray they decide to lead us."

The man pulled the floppy hat from his head and said, "I'm with Harker." He turned toward Carson and Gate. "I for one would appreciate it if you agreed to lead us."

An hour later, Carson, Bella, Gate, and the girls ate Maria's spicy goat stew on warm corn tortillas. Each had a glass of goat buttermilk to cool the burn from the peppers.

Gate stood and said, "Come on girls, let's go check on the horses."

Liliana moaned. "I want to stay."

Bella smiled at her and said, "Go on with Mr. Rudd. Carson and I need to talk."

Liliana set her elbows on the table and grinned. "I wanna talk too."

Bella slid her fingers through the girl's dark hair. "Go on. I'll be out to tuck you in."

As the girls left, Gate touched Carson's shoulder. "Whatever y'all decide's fine with me."

Carson glanced around the room. The old Mexican stood at the bar, talking to Maria. There were half a dozen men from the wagon train at each of two tables, drinking beer and laughing. He turned to Bella, still not knowing what to say.

Bella smiled and looked him in the eyes. "What are you going to do, Deputy?"

Carson shrugged and shook his head. "Gate's got the money, Mr. Van Zant left you."

She attempted a smile and swallowed. "I'm grateful for that. It'll give me and the girls a little independence."

Carson nodded, but he wondered what that meant for him. He looked past her at the door. "What do you want?"

"I asked first," she said with a sassy grin.

"I don't know. Depends on..." He looked into her eyes. "I need to know..." The words stuck in his throat. "I need to go to Denver and collect the reward money for the Whatleys, but I suppose there's no rush for that." He looked at the card-playing men. "Trying to keep these people in line's like herding cats..., but unless Gate, or maybe one of the army scouts, shows them the way, they're in trouble."

"I know it's not right, but part of me wants them to suffer," she said.

"Me too," Carson said, "but Mr. Van Zant promised to get you all to California, and I'd like to make sure that happens. Not for them, but for him. Gate doesn't think he's got the patience to deal with the squabbling, and if I don't go, he's not going."

Bella laughed. "Sounds like you need to go."

He nodded, then not looking around or caring who might see, he reached over and laid his hand on hers.

She looked down at the table, then met his eyes. "California was my father's dream, not mine. It sounds beautiful, but if it's full of people like these," she glanced out toward the wagons. "I'm not sure I want to go there."

"There's good and bad people everywhere." He thought of his friend Ernie. "And sometimes bad people see the light."

She nodded.

"Where would you go?"

She shrugged. "Suppose one place is as good or as bad as another."

He squeezed her hand. "Come back to Fort Smith with me."

She shook her head. "I can't go backwards."

He let go of her hand and slid back in his chair.

Before he could pull his hand away. She grabbed it and pulled him toward her. "Maria," she called over the laughter from the drinking men. She pointed to their empty glasses.

As Maria went into the back for the pitcher of buttermilk, Bella followed her with a faraway look in her eyes.

Marie brought the pitcher and refilled their glasses.

Bella pulled out a chair. "Sit for a minute."

Maria hesitated, then sat.

"How long have you been here?" Bella asked.

"Most of my life," Maria said. "Mr. Jesse...," She laughed. "He wasn't so old then, lost his wife, and he came to love my momma."

"Did they marry?"

Maria shook her head.

"What's going to happen to all this?"

"I suppose Randall will sell it. He hates this place."

"Randall?" Bella asked.

"Mr. Jesse's son. He's a doctor in Houston."

"Will you buy it?"

Maria pulled out the lining of her dress pocket and smiled a sad smile.

"What will you do?" Bella asked.

Maria glanced out the window. "Might go to El Paso." She glanced at Carson. "This is the only home I remember."

Bella looked out the window, past the wagons, and toward the Concho River. "It is beautiful. Seems with the soldiers for protection and the rivers coming together, this Santa Angela is a place with a future, maybe a place a person could start over."

Carson glanced from Bella to Maria and back. Where was she going with this?

"What if you had a partner?" Bella asked.

Carson pulled his hand from under Bella's. What did she mean?

Maria's eyes opened wide. "What do you mean? Who?"

Bella glanced at Carson, then turned back to Maria. "I just came into some money. I wonder how much Randall would take for it all?"

~

I HOPE you enjoyed Carson Kettle Book 4. You can order book 5 in the series at: http://readerlinks.com/l/1888821.

AFTERWORD

July 15, 2021

Once again, here we are at the end of another Carson Kettle book. Thank you all for reading another of my books.!

I'm writing this little afterward, sitting in the shade on the porch. When I look up from the computer screen, I'm blessed to see my old rope horse, standing in the shade of a big old pine tree, switching his tail at flies. Behind him, a rugged, rocky ridge stretches across the horizon from north to south as far as I can see.

I'm listening to Robert Earl Keen sing "The Road Goes On Forever," and in a few minutes, I'm going to take a break and watch the Calgary Stampede on television.

It's been hot and dry here this summer. Great weather for making hay, but now the forest fires are starting, and we could sure use a good rain. It's been smoky, but today the wind is blowing from the west and the air is clear and clean.

It's a great day to be alive.

Carson and Bella both have big decisions to make.

Bella's living day to day and following her gut. Something feels right about Santa Angela (today's San Angelo), the little village growing up on the confluence of the North, South, and Middle Concho Rivers, but her primary focus is on the girls.

Carson's learning to track, shoot, and lead people, but he's still struggling to find the words to tell Bella how he feels, and he's got 'miles to go' and 'promises to keep.' He could follow his heart and stay with Bella and the girls in Santa Angela. Or he could finish the job Mr. Van Zant started and lead the wagon train west to California. Before too long, he needs to go to Denver and collect the reward money for the Whatleys.

He and I are both still figuring out where he's going. I do know he ends up, years later, as the U.S. Marshal in Denver, with Marty Dunnegan as his chief deputy, so I guess I'll just keep following him until he gets there.

I hope and pray that my note finds you and yours healthy and happy.

Until next time,

Wyatt

ABOUT THE AUTHOR

Hey there, I'm Wyatt Cochrane. Once I've enjoyed some time roping and riding, I love to write stories. I enjoy a good tale, and I'm devoted to giving my readers fast-paced, life-or-death Western adventures.

I love to throw hay over the fence to a good rope horse, and I've felt the tug on the reins when a powerful team of draft horses leans into their collars to start a heavy load.

I've carried a gun to uphold the law, and I've grappled with the rights and wrongs of deadly force. I try to weave these feelings, sights, sounds, and smells into my stories.

I love strong men and women who overcome insurmountable odds, and I always hope they find love. I enjoy hearing from readers, so please visit me at Wyatt Cochrane

Printed in Great Britain
by Amazon